Mara's Legacy

by

Z. Minor

The Sisterhood of the Coin, Book 2

Mara's Legacy

Cover Art by *Debbie Taylor*

The Wild Rose Press, Inc.
PO Box 708
Adams Basin, NY 14410-0708
Visit us at www.thewildrosepress.com

Publishing History
First Tea Rose Edition, 2019
Print ISBN 978-1-5092-2469-2
Digital ISBN 978-1-5092-2470-8

The Sisterhood of the Coin, Book 2
Published in the United States of America

He had fallen in love the first time they met. She was everything Barnaby wanted in a woman. Mara was only a few inches shorter than his six feet four inches. His brown hair looked even darker when compared to Mara's threads of spun gold curls. Her hands were delicate, and her long fingers elegant. He became mesmerized watching her hands move as she talked.

But he knew he would never be able to make an offer for her hand. He had no title, no estate, and not nearly enough money. Most importantly, however, it would not be an advantageous match for her. He was a former thief from the East End of London, while she had connections to London's high society.

He heard the commotion, looked ahead, and quit his daydreaming. He bolted down the street without even thinking the moment he recognized Mara. He silently approached the man from behind and slammed him to the ground. The pistol slid across the pavement stopping inches from the boys.

"Do not touch the weapon," Mara ordered them.

Barnaby grasped the front of the attacker's coat, jerked him to his feet, and managed to get in a solid punch. The man staggered then spun around in a circle.

"Back to the shop with her," Barnaby shouted to the boys. He pulled a blackjack from his back pocket.

Praise for Z. Minor

"Minor's story is filled with wonderful characters, intrigue, and interesting historical tidbits. I highly recommend this second book in the 'Sisterhood of the Coin' series."

~Bonnie Tharp, Award-winning Author

~*~

"Wonderful story, great characters. A must read."

~Kathy Pritchett, Author

Dedication

To John, my knight in shining armor.
Without you, there would be no me.

Acknowledgments

There are many people to thank for making my book a reality: Jean Dusenberry, Bonnie Tharp, Rae Cuda, Kathy Pritchett, and Susan Wilczek. Your comments and friendships are more help than you will ever know.

Thanks to my wonderful, patient editor Anne. There are not enough words to show my appreciation for the time you have spent making my book the best it can be, despite my errors, and keeping it true to the historical past.

Chapter One

Woodhaven Manor, 1821, London

Mara Highbridge, the mistress of detail, mulled over her strategy even in her dreams. Give her an idea, and in no time, she formulated a plan for its completion from start to finish; nothing ever was left to chance.

Before going downstairs to surprise her older sister with an impromptu meeting, two words popped into her mind—positive thinking. She had to keep her emotions hidden. Theatrics would not help her cause. Mara worried her lip. She did not have time to devise a new scheme. It was time for action. Her future depended on her sister agreeing to her plan.

She hoped to convince Nicola for the very first time in their lives that she, Mara, could and would take charge, and follow through with a plan of action without anyone's help. She only needed to obtain some information from Nicola's mother. A shiver flowed through her entire body when Mara realized she would be at the forefront, not hiding behind the scenes as was her usual strategy.

She walked out of her bedroom and took a deep breath. Mara straightened out the dark blue ribbons cascading down the front of her new dress. She stuck out her left shoe and then the right to make sure there were no smudges on her new dark blue leather slippers.

To keep the cold draft off her back, she draped her shawl over her shoulders and strolled down the stairs as she gathered her courage.

Mara took a sneak peek in the hall mirror to make sure her curls were gathered on the top of her head and tiny tendrils were in place around her face. Looking her best just might make a difference in the outcome of her encounter.

Nicola had been her champion her entire life. Mara was always the quiet, organized, determined one. She never ruffled anyone's feathers. She left that task to her dear sister—and irritate them her older sister did from time to time. This allowed Mara to sit back, look innocent, and let her sister fight her battles—large and small. Yet all would change today if her plans moved forward as she hoped.

Mara's head pounded just thinking about it as she stood ready to intercept her sister. Nicola was leaving the city for an undetermined duration. There would not be much time to plead her case.

The second Mara heard her sister's voice, she hurried to the foot of the stairs in the foyer and began biting her nails.

This is my last chance to convince Nicola to get the information only her dear mother can provide. I can do this; I can do this. I know I can do this.

The moment her sister's feet touched the tiled floor, Mara cleared her throat as she strolled up to her. "Sister-Dear, before you leave I must speak to you." Her mouth suddenly dry, she found it hard to swallow. How Mara wished for a cup of hot tea. "It is important—at least to me."

"Now? We are ready to depart. The carriage"—

Nicola pointed to the front entrance—"has arrived."

Mara pursed her lips. "I promise to take but a moment of your time. Please, Sister-Dear." She walked over to the library doors, opened them, tapped her right foot, and watched her sister and brother-in-law.

Nicola turned to her husband and handed him her coat. "Clay, I shall be a moment."

"Take your time." He squeezed her hand and spoke just loud enough for Mara to hear. "You know she is up to something."

"Yes, the moment she said, 'Sister-Dear.' "

To keep from being disturbed Mara shut the library door after her sister crossed the threshold. "I promise to be brief." She reached into her side pocket and produced the old Roman coin with a chariot on its face and her name engraved on the back. Mara passed it to Nicola.

"I am invoking the pledge we made when The Sisterhood of the Coin began so many years ago. I am requesting you gather information about my birth parents and any pertinent details about the person or persons who delivered me to your mother, my foster mother, when I was only days old."

Mara held up her hands to stop her sister from interrupting. "Please let me continue." She shut her eyes for a moment. She could not lose her nerve when she had come this far.

"I have thought about this since your discovery of your birth parents. I need to know why *my* parents gave me away like a loaf of bread. My birth family may not have a position in society like yours. However, it has become all I think about since hearing those women talking at Mrs. Pearly's party late last year. I must know who and what they are, even if they are not the most desirable."

"I don't know what my mother can or will tell you or me. You must remember she is gravely ill and that is the reason Clay and I are leaving now for Highbridge Manor."

"All I request is that you talk to her. Ask her to share any details about the night I was brought to her. This might be my last opportunity to gather any information. She is the only one who holds the key to my beginnings."

"I pray my mother's illness shall pass. And I shall honor our pledge made so long ago. I accept your coin and promise to do all I can to assist. After all, isn't that what sisters do?"

"Thank you, Sister—"

"Do not call me Sister-Dear again. You and Emmy only use that endearment when you expect me to take on one of your problems. Well, not this time. I can only gather relevant facts for you. Do with them what you wish. Remember, I cannot come to help you."

The two women hugged as Clay knocked on the door. "Nicola, we must leave."

Mara strolled back into the library after the carriage vanished down the street. She sat in front of the fire. Once the information pointed her in the right direction, it would be time to face reality. She would have to ask the questions that needed to be asked, and be strong enough, and smart enough to seek not only the answers but take any necessary action as well. Mara's nerves were strung tighter than she could have ever imagined.

****

The following evening, Mara parted the lace curtains covering the glass front door of her dress shop. She took one look at the darkening sky and decided she could not get a hansom cab to stop due to the increase in traffic. It would be faster to walk the short distance to the Woodhaven Estate. The wind picked up the leaves near the lamp post, swirling them across the sidewalk in front of the shop. Mara slipped on her coat and wrapped her multi-colored woven scarf tightly around her neck. She pulled on her gloves, stepped outside into the cold air, then shut and locked the door behind her.

The lamplighter jumped from his ladder to the pavement. She wished him a pleasant evening. He tipped his hat, gathered his toolbox, swung his ladder onto his shoulder, and scurried down the street. Until her sister and brother-in-law returned, Mara was house minding the Woodhaven Estate. She would be the lady of the manor, a thought which caused her to hum a happy tune.

Except for the road traffic, the street was void of people. The light from the street lamps flickered, darkening the shadows around the buildings. Without warning, a gust of wind danced the leaves and dust across the pavement, first going one way and then another. She wanted to cross the road at the corner where vehicles were forced to stop for traffic entering the main road. Mara set a brisk pace toward the edge of her shop.

Suddenly a chorus of voices permeated the air. "Miss Mara! Miss Mara! You forgots your hat."

She turned toward the sound of thundering feet. Eel, her store manager's son, and his mates dashed to catch up to her. Without warning, she found herself facing in the opposite direction. A man gripped her upper arm and pulled her closer to him.

"Now!" His deep voice growled, "You be coming with me."

She looked straight into his dark, blood-shot eyes. Mara tripped on the hem of her dress and staggered. He was dragging her away from Creations. The smell of rotting cabbage permeated the air. Greasy hair framed his pockmarked face. His black coat danced around him when the wind caught the unbuttoned garment. An angry scar crisscrossed the top of his hand.

"You let me go, right now!" Mara shrieked, straining to dislodge his fingers. "Who are you?" She pounded on his hand with her clenched fist. She struggled to yank her arm out of her coat sleeve. His grip proved too tight. Her legs continued to get tangled in her skirt.

"I refuse to go anywhere with the likes of you." She spun, twisted to break loose, and knocked the top hat from his head.

Chapter Two

Eel and his mates slid to a stop inches from Mara. Eel grabbed the man's forearm, trying to maneuver his body between them. Jeb, one of Eel's mates, aimed a hard kick at the attacker's shins. The moment Jeb made contact he bellowed. Jimmy, the third boy in the trio, stuck his foot out to trip the gent. The lad stumbled against Mara.

Eel observed the attacker trying to pull Mara toward the back of the building next to the dress shop. Jeb continued to kick at the man's shins and made direct contact more than once. The lads danced away from the gent's colossal swinging arm and managed to keep the man and Mara in front of the shop.

"Lady, come now or I shoot." He suddenly pulled a pistol from his coat pocket.

The three lads tried their best to stand in front of Mara. Each time they did, she stepped in front of them. "You boys stay behind me," she shouted.

The attacker continued to wave the pistol in Mara's and then the lads' direction. "I kill you all now."

****

Barnaby Roget, a family friend and a partner of Mara's brother-in-law, found himself strolling by Creations most days in the hope he would get a glimpse of her or possibly even talk to her. He had fallen in love the first time they met. She was everything Barnaby wanted in a woman. Mara was only a few inches shorter than his six feet four inches. His brown hair looked even darker when compared to Mara's threads of spun gold curls. Her hands were delicate, and her long fingers elegant. He became mesmerized watching her hands move as she talked.

But he knew he would never be able to make an offer for her hand. He had no title, no estate, and not nearly enough money. Most importantly, however, it would not be an advantageous match for her. He was a former thief from the East End of London, while she had connections to London's high society.

He heard the commotion, looked ahead, and quit his daydreaming. He bolted down the street without even thinking the moment he recognized Mara. He silently approached the man from behind and slammed him to the ground. The pistol slid across the pavement, stopping inches from the boys.

"Do not touch the weapon," Mara ordered them.

Barnaby grasped the front of the attacker's coat, jerked him to his feet, and managed to get in a solid punch. The man staggered then spun around in a circle.

"Back to the shop with her," Barnaby shouted to the boys. He pulled a blackjack from his back pocket.

The attacker dashed across the sidewalk. He darted into the bustling traffic. Shouts of alarm from the carriage drivers followed him across the road.

Susan, the store manager, opened the shop door seconds before Mara and the lads vanished behind it. Barnaby reached down to pick up the weapon and Mara's hat leaning on the lamp post. He rushed after them. When Barnaby entered the building, the silence was unnerving after the scuffle on the street.

"Mara, where are you?" he called.

Susan entered the room. "Please to follow me. Her be settled in the final fitting room."

Barnaby followed. He rubbed the sore knuckles on his right hand. Mara sat with her head tilted against the back of an upholstered loveseat. Her eyes were closed. He knelt down and took her folded, cold hands into his. Her hands trembled. He felt her racing pulse.

"My dear, are you hurt?" he whispered. He inhaled deeply. Mara's rose perfume floated around him. He felt the heat of his yearning and reached out to touch her hair.

She licked her lips and shook her head. "I am still in one piece, though a little shaken. I have no idea what happened or why."

He liked the soft feel of her hands, enjoyed holding and stroking them, even if it wasn't proper. He appreciated the comfort it gave him. Barnaby wanted to take her in his arms and keep her close.

Susan carried in a chair for him.

"Where is Eel?" Barnaby never took his eyes off Mara. "He must go and bring Clay and Nicola." He leaned back in his chair. "It is not safe for Mara to be on her own."

"They be gone. Left London yesterday."

His shoulders slumped. "Oh, how could I have forgotten?"

"They plan to be gone at least for a fortnight. I am staying at Woodhaven until they return," Mara whispered.

Susan poured freshly made tea into cups for Barnaby and Mara. The fragrant smell of mint filled the air.

"When I saw the pistol, I did not know what to do—he could have…"

When her hand started to shake, Barnaby gently took the cup and set it on the table next to the loveseat.

"I have never been so scared. I am so thankful you were there. Without you, I do not know what would have happened to us." Mara shuddered and closed her eyes.

"Who is staying with you at Woodhaven?" Barnaby retook her hand and squeezed it.

"Susan, Eel, and the servants. So, you see, I am not alone."

"I shall stay in some corner of the house until we discover who is responsible for tonight's disturbance. I promise not to compromise you in any way. A crazy man tried to kill you tonight. I cannot leave you on your own."

Barnaby wrote a note asking the butler to have the carriage brought to Creations. It would not be safe for Mara to walk the short distance to her temporary home. Eel and his mates thundered out of the shop with the paper tucked securely in Eel's pocket.

In no time the carriage sat in the mews at the back of the shop. The lads returned with two Bow Street Runners. The two burly men entered Creations behind the boys. One Runner stayed to guard the dress shop. One would be their escort to Woodhaven. Barnaby would have to arrange for other bodyguards. Rather than be gone this night, he would go see an old friend in the early morning hours. Tonight, it was necessary to get everyone settled in the house.

Mara started to fall asleep about the time the carriage came to a complete stop in front of

Woodhaven. The lads jumped down. Barnaby surveyed the street. Once he felt it was safe, Susan and Mara exited the coach. The Runner stood off to the side ready to spring into action if needed. Once the inside of the house had been secured, the Runner would patrol the outside until daybreak.

A comfortable fire always burned in the library, which kept the constant draft out of the large room, which for some reason no one could explain had become the official gathering place in the home. The double doors opened inward. The fireplace stood left of the entrance. A bank of three windows along the outside wall overlooked the garden. Bookshelves covered the remaining walls and accommodated every size of book imaginable from the smallest, the size of a man's palm, to the bulkiest, which required two people to move. A large desk stood on the far side of the room. Chairs and a loveseat sat in a semi-circle before the fire.

"We be having our evening meal with the servants." Susan took charge of the boys.

"Thank you. Mr. Barnaby and I plan to eat here. We have much to discuss." Mara walked over and sat in one of the chairs and draped her shawl around her feet. "I am so tired." She yawned. "Please excuse me. Believe me, it is not the company." She leaned her head against the back of the chair.

Barnaby cleared his throat. "Are you sure you did not see your attacker in the past? I do not believe he would have been hard to miss. Maybe one of your customer's servants or a man on the street?"

"I have never seen him until tonight. I may forget someone's name but never a face. I do not deal directly with any of Creations' customers."

"Not ever?"

"Never. Being the owner and couturière of a dress shop is my best-kept secret. If anyone knew, I would no longer be invited to social functions. I would be considered a shop owner, which is little better than a servant to many in the upper crust of society."

"Who handles your clients?" Barnaby stood and walked over to the bottles of liquor on the sideboard. "Do you mind if I pour myself a whiskey?"

"Help yourself." Mara reached out toward the handsome man. "Please bring one to me too."

"Would you rather have a sherry? I could ring the bell for the butler or a maid."

"No. I want a whiskey. Sherry is for old ladies."

"Yes, miss. One whiskey for the lady." Barnaby poured two drinks and handed one to her with a slight bow. "Do you think you should contact Nicola and Clay about your attack tonight? They would most likely return."

"I cannot do that. Nicola would come back and take over as she always does when one of her sisters has a problem. I believe it is time to stand on my own and learn to take care of myself. Besides, they did not go for just a visit. Her mother is ill. Nicola waited her entire life to find her parents. She should spend time with them before it is too late and they are gone forever."

"Then the duchess's illness is serious?"

"The physician is not sure what is amiss, and that is the reason they have gone to Highbridge Manor. Nicola is a herbalist and a healer in her own right. The physician is the best in the country. I believe in no time they will solve the mystery of her illness."

"You mentioned your sister Emmy. Do you think we need to worry about her?"

"She currently is out in the English countryside on one of her searches for her ancient ones."

"Ancient ones?"

"Emmy's interests are in anyone who lived long, long ago. Many landowners have given her permission to dig for ancient artifacts on their property since she moved to London. Anything she discovers goes to the British Museum. She was studying archaeology long before it became popular. I must admit it is rather fascinating and is beginning to pique people's interest and of course mine. Just do not tell her I said so."

The couple ate dinner in silence. Susan entered after knocking to announce she and the lads were off to bed. They agreed to go to the dress shop at the same time in the morning. Barnaby requested a tour of Creations and announced he would hire bodyguards to watch over the ladies and the shop during the day. He promised to come and escort everyone back to Woodhaven when Creations closed. Barnaby knew it wasn't going to be easy to solve this mystery that had landed at his feet. He just had to turn over the right rock to discover who and why someone had been trying to hurt his Mara.

Before entering his sleeping quarters in the back of the manor house, Barnaby suddenly stopped and leaned against the wall. Was Mara, he wondered, holding something back?

Chapter Three

Barnaby lay awake most of the night. Up until now, he had been in a two-man partnership with Mara's brother-in-law. The two men were a team and usually tackled any problem together. They even worked for the government on occasion. This time Barnaby would be handling everything on his own. It made him uncomfortable and a bit nervous. What if he made the wrong decision? Mara's life was at stake.

Long before daybreak Barnaby left the house to hire four bodyguards—two per shift and two shifts for each day. One was to watch the shop and one to look after Mara. He went to the magistrate to engage four Bow Street Runners. Usually, the Runners only worked for a citizen of London on their time off. Barnaby hoped this would be considered an extraordinary case. He did find it necessary to mention Mara's connection to the Duke of Russellton and Earl of Woodhaven. Barnaby agreed to pay the Runners' regular salary plus ten percent directly to the magistrate.

The three men hurried back to the house and walked into the library where Mara had just sat down to breakfast. He introduced the Runners, explained what they would be doing and that two other Runners would have the evening shift.

With raised eyebrows, Mara sat her napkin down next to her plate. "Is this necessary?"

"I am afraid it is. I want everyone to be safe. Until I can gather more information, we all must be vigilant."

The taller of the two Runners said, "We be ever watchful over you, Miss Highbridge."

The three lads rushed in through the opened door. Eel's mother Susan hurried behind them.

"We be ready, Miss Mara." Eel stood in the doorway. "We got school today. I did promise 'er ladyship we'd be attending every day. 'Er promised to…" Eel frowned.

"If I am not mistaken, upon returning she plans to quiz you." Mara nodded her head.

"You be right, just could not 'member it."

"Go and request Mrs. Millbe make a mid-day meal for each of you. We will all leave as soon as you return."

The boys scampered out of the room. Their footsteps resounded down the hallway.

"Do they ever walk? Just listening to them wears me out." Mara shook her head. "Susan, how do you manage?"

"They do be a handful at times. I be off to 'elp cook." Susan turned to the door.

Barnaby sat next to Mara. "Today when you are at the shop I would like you to make a list of anyone you believe might be responsible for engaging the man. It took me a long time to fall asleep last night. I checked all the doors and windows a minimum of six times before I convinced myself no one could gain entry. I believe someone thinks you have something that they want. They will do whatever it takes to possess it."

"I am happy to do as requested. But the list will be short. You see, I do not know many people in London and have only been going to social affairs for the past three months. Before the *Ton* heard of Nicola and her new-found family, we—Nicola, Emmy, and I—were country folk with no family history. Emmy and I still don't have a family other than our foster mother. Now since she is married, we have acquired a foster father, who just happens to be the Duke of Russellton."

"That may be, but there has to be something or someone. Tonight, we shall figure it all out. I do not think it will prove a difficult task once we put our minds to it. My experience is the answer is always the obvious one. It is just a process of elimination."

The sound of thundering feet announced the return of the lads. They could hear Susan telling them to be quiet, but they did not listen. A knock on the door proclaimed their arrival and a short argument as to who would have the honor of announcing them. Eel won like he always did. He was the leader; Jimmy and Jeb were his mates. The three of them were most often together.

"Enter." Mara stood. "We are ready to leave. Hirsch can have the carriage brought around."

"Oh, miss, it be a very grand day. Could we walk?" Eel's feet never stopped moving.

"Mr. Barnaby can make the decision." Mara reached for her coat lying across one of the chairs. "It does sound like a good plan to me. Creations is not far."

"If we can stay together in a group and you lads listen to me. Someone is trying to harm Miss Mara. We must protect her." Barnaby walked to the library door. "Do you think you can do that?"

"Yes, Mr. Barnaby," they said in unison and then giggled.

Barnaby strolled to the front door after Hirsch, the

butler, handed him his coat. They left the house and walked down the street. Few people were about due to the early hour. Barnaby and one of the Runners led the way. The lads moved in behind the women, and the other Runner followed them. They strolled around to the back door of the shop. Barnaby waited with Mara in the final dressing room. Susan and the Runners did a complete search of the dress shop and Susan and Eel's living quarters.

They heard the three people go up the stairs to the living quarters. There were two bedrooms, a small sitting room with a fireplace, and a kitchen with a table in the center. A large number of windows made the rooms seem more substantial, especially when sunlight filled the area.

Barnaby and Mara didn't realize Susan and the men had re-entered the room until Susan spoke.

"Miss Mara, no one entered the shop. Before we left last night, I wove some thread around the chairs and table legs. If anyone done come in, the thread would be broken. All me little traps are just like I left them."

"Susan, good thinking. No one is to leave Creations without an escort. At no time is Miss Mara to be left on her own. I have some business to attend to and shall be back as soon as possible. Are there any questions?"

"There be no need for us to leave, but if we must?" the taller Runner asked.

"Then you best hire someone you know and trust with your life"—Barnaby turned and looked directly at the men—"because if anything happens to anyone in your care, I promise to find you. England isn't big enough for you to hide in. Do I make myself clear?"

"Yes, sir." Both men stared at Barnaby and nodded their heads.

Barnaby hurried out the back door. He needed help, but knew of only one man in London he could, and would trust. The big question was would he assist his old friend?

It didn't take Barnaby long to reach the Black Rose Pub. The building hadn't changed. The sign always needed to be repainted. The windows were still caked with dirt and grime. He would not be surprised if some of the dust were in place long before he was born. Barnaby grimaced.

He stopped, looked at the people on the road. Barnaby shuddered to think about the last time he had been here. Rather than bring those memories to the forefront of his mind, he took a deep breath of clean outside air and quietly opened the door. The smell of unwashed bodies, stale liquor, and cheap perfume swirled around the second the outer door closed. He managed to force down his stomach contents every time it tried to creep up his throat. The years fell away. It was as if he hadn't left this place. He did not have good memories of the East End. His old feelings had not changed. He hated it then. He hated it now.

Barnaby heard his friend's voice long before he saw Graham holding court at the back bar. The lighting was dim, which made it difficult to see. All he could do was follow the sound of the voices. Nothing inside the pub had changed. Just like in the old days, a crowd of men of all ages sat around Graham and listened to his every word. In days gone by, Graham's father had been the one holding court. He had been dead for a good long time. Barnaby and the old man had gotten along for the most part.

Now was not the time to interrupt his friend. Barnaby leaned up against a post, lit a cigar and paid for a pint. Graham walked toward him.

"Follow me," he whispered as he passed Barnaby.

There are some things you never forget and these two words, 'Follow me,' had a double or triple meaning. Trouble could be brewing, or Graham didn't want anyone to realize he knew Barnaby. There was always the possibility something was happening at this very moment. Graham couldn't speak of it when others could hear him. In fact, it could be all three, so Barnaby casually strolled behind his old friend.

Graham moved behind a massive painted screen of a nude woman. He produced a key and opened a door. Graham motioned Barnaby through another door and down a short hallway into a large sitting room, which faced a courtyard and the back of a house.

Barnaby's height gave him a view of the outside structure and allowed him to see above the fence separating the areas. The room reeked of old, musty, and moldy food and dirty clothes. The stuffing was falling out of the only two cushioned chairs near the windows in the corner. Scarred dining room chairs sat around a lopsided table. A rug lay half-haphazard underneath it, so old and worn he could count the bare threads.

"I could not be sure you still kept hours here. Looks like nothing much changed since the old days." Barnaby ran his fingers through his hair.

"Most mornings I can be found here. This is the only place people come looking for me. You made me quit thieving but..." The man nodded his head.

"…sometimes they need me. Cannot be turning away old friends."

"You get much action?" Barnaby re-lit his cigar.

"Not so much now. I keep a watch for interlopers. You know the kind, trying to weasel onto our street, our lives, and take advantage of the old players." He ran his hand across his lower jaw. "Nowadays I keep a lookout and make sure the right people are aware of what is happening. Just enough to enjoy myself iffin' you know what I mean." Graham reached out and slapped Barnaby on the back.

"Why do you think I came to you? A situation is surfacing, and the consequences could be deadly. I need to locate a few able-bodied men who can assist me. They have to know the underground of the East End and be honest above all."

"I am not sure what or who might crawl out of the woodwork in this place. Let us leave and find a proper place to talk." Graham nodded his head.

"Then why do you stay?" Barnaby grabbed his friend's arm.

"Come with me." Graham turned. He went up the stairs, and Barnaby followed his friend without hesitation.

The men walked through another door and down a long hallway. Graham stood back and pushed opened the second door with his foot. He motioned Barnaby to step ahead of him. The smell of freshly baked bread wafted around him. Barnaby glanced back at his friend as he continued to walk further into the room. Unless he missed his guess, this could only be the building next door and where Graham lived.

A beautiful woman engulfed Barnaby in a hug.

"Oh my, look who is here for a visit. How are you?"

Barnaby stepped back, "Maggie, is it really you?"

"No one else would marry Graham. I took pity on him all them years ago." Maggie placed a teapot on the table. "Care for some fresh tea, bread, and jam? Just like your ma baked for us. You know she taught me well."

"Remember how we all survived on old bread, minus the mold we cut off one winter?" Graham announced. "I can still see us stuffing our faces."

"How did we ever survive those early years?" Barnaby shook his head.

"Well, I just made bread. So, let us eat up, and you can tell us why you have come." Maggie set a plate of freshly cut bread, butter, and homemade jam on the table.

While they ate, Barnaby told them about Mara and the problem he found himself in. "So, you see, I need both of you to help. We have to have enough men to guard Miss Mara and her shop, plus her store manager and three lads—actually, street urchins in every sense of the word."

"Do you happen to mean Eel, Jimmy, and Jeb?" Maggie raised her eyebrows.

"How did you—?"

"Everyone knows them, and Eel knows everyone, including Maggie and me."

"I should have known. Well, I have four Runners, two working day hours and two working nights. I need more honest men. Clay Barber is out of town, so I am on my own. Tonight, Miss Mara and I are having a meeting. I would like you both to join us."

"Is there somewhere on the estate where three to

four men could live without being noticed? They could take turns being bodyguards while you go about your business." Graham touched his fingertips together. "I can, in the meantime, hit the streets, listen to the gossip and the talk being bantered about. How do I reach you?"

"After hours, come to the Woodhaven Estate. Go to the north back door, and I will notify the butler—his name is Hirsch—to find me or tell you where I am." Barnaby leaned toward the couple. "I would rather we keep our activities to ourselves. It is best if no one knows what we are about."

"We can do that." Graham licked some jelly off his lips. "Just like old times."

"Maggie, do you think you could come and chaperone Mara?" Barnaby rubbed the back of his neck. "I actually believe our problem will be solved soon."

"You care that much about her?" Maggie touched his arm.

"Yes, I do. I might not ever be able to marry her. However, I would never compromise Mara."

"Why could you not marry her?" Maggie frowned.

"I—"

"Listen, your love life or lack of one is your business and yours alone. I can bring Maggie to the estate in time for the evening meal." Graham clapped Barnaby on the back. "It will provide an excellent opportunity for us all to get acquainted. We have plans to make."

"How will I ever be able to thank you both?"

"Thank us? If you had not helped us all those years ago, I would most likely be dead." Graham put his hands in his pockets. "Maggie would be living in Australia or the colonies. We owe you our lives."

Maggie reached out and hugged Barnaby. Graham shook his hand. Then he showed Barnaby the proper way to leave and enter their home.

Not for one minute did Barnaby think Mara's problem was going to fade away without mishap. His old gang would have to keep their wits about them as they moved deeper into the underbelly of the East End. There was no doubt where all this was headed. He hoped they would be able to gather some details this evening which would start his investigation into the problems Mara faced. He jammed his hands into his pockets and pulled up his collar as he left his old stomping grounds behind him.

Chapter Four

Barnaby hastened back to Creations. He leaned on the lamp post, counted and scrutinized the people who entered and left the shop. When the last lady and her escort departed, Barnaby opened the front door. He walked into the main salon and stood silently. Women were still gathered around the room. It took just a few seconds for him to notice no one moved or spoke. He scratched his head.

Did I count wrong? Or miscounted when I happened to be daydreaming about my Mara.

His curiosity got the best of him. Finally, he walked closer to a woman with a fur coat draped over her arm, and then a little closer to one dressed in a beautiful evening gown.

There is no way two women could stand together and not be talking.

Barnaby shook his head. They all were life-like statues standing not far from the doorway. He reached out his hand to touch one just as Susan came into the room. He dropped his arm to his side.

"Mara made them. One of the patrons said the mannequins were…Oh, I cannot 'member the word." Susan chewed on her lip. "I know they be…amazing. Yes, that be the word—amazing. At times, I forget they ain't real."

Having never been in a woman's clothing shop,

Barnaby found interest in everything. He continued to survey the green painted room. Clustered around the room were small tables and chairs. Fashion plates filled a countertop on the back wall. A bolt of pale purple material lay across the end of a table top close to him. He extended his fingers and ran them across the soft fabric.

Susan stood in the doorway and motioned him into a pale-yellow showroom. A large mirror hung on the wall directly across from a platform, which sat in the middle of the room. A smaller set of three mirrors was anchored in a movable frame.

"I see you be looking at another of Miss Mara's inventions. Our patrons love them movable mirrors. They can see themselves from every direction." Susan thrust her shoulders back. "Not many shops be having such a grand tool. I be sure it has increased Creations' sales."

A small portable table on wheels sat pushed to one side of the platform. Pins had fallen onto the floor while a tape measure cascaded down the front. Susan turned to the left. They walked into a fitting room. Through a small doorway in the back of the chamber, Barnaby could see clothes on some type of wire hanger.

They turned to the right and walked toward a stairway. "My living quarters be up the stairs. Do you wish to see 'em?"

"Not at this time, maybe later or another day."

She walked toward the first step, turned left, and knocked on a door. When it opened, one of the Runners stood in the opening and moved forward.

"I do think it best if I come out there." Mara maneuvered herself out of the room. "There is not enough space for us in my office. Susan is going to make us tea, which we shall have in one of the fitting rooms."

Both men followed Mara. Within minutes, Susan had tea and biscuits ready for them.

The Runner politely refused any refreshments, gave his report and left for the day. He promised to be back at the house before daybreak tomorrow to watch over Mara and the shop. Eel and his mates showed up within minutes of Barnaby returning. There were no late appointments, so everyone walked to Woodhaven.

The lads sat down to do their studying in the kitchen while Susan helped prepare the supper meal. Barnaby informed Mrs. Millbe, the cook, there would be guests for the evening meal.

"How many people should I be planning for?"

"There will be two."

"Very well." Mrs. Millbe left the room.

"Who have you invited to dinner, Mr. Barnaby?"

"Would you please call me Barnaby, and I will call you Mara? After all, we are living in the same house."

"It is not proper. You should be aware of the impropriety." Mara frowned.

"At least when we are alone," Barnaby stated.

"I see your point." Mara sighed. "Tell me who your guests are."

"Graham and Maggie Rogers. They have been friends of mine since my childhood. Graham and I were in the same gang in the East End," he added. "When Maggie became an orphan, my mother took her in so she would not have to live on the streets. I asked Maggie to stay in the house and be your chaperone while I am here."

"I do not need someone to watch over me." Mara's eyes narrowed. "What if I do not like this woman called Maggie?"

"Not like her? That would be impossible. She is the nicest, kindest person and married Graham. She is not afraid of anything."

"Yes, but—"

"No 'but' anything. You cannot stay by yourself. It is not safe for one thing, and Susan does not count. She is employed by you. I have to be here. I promise not to compromise you in any way. If anyone from the *Ton* should find you and me staying in the same house by ourselves, you would never be able to hold your head up in society."

"I believe it is for me to decide—not you."

"Think again. If Maggie does not stay here, I shall send for Nicola and Clay. It is your choice, miss." Barnaby turned and walked out.

****

I am going to strangle him. Who does he think he is? Telling me what I can and cannot do. Mara sighed deeply. *I may have no choice in the matter. He doesn't need to tell me so!*

She leaned against the chair, closed her eyes, and fell sound asleep. She dreamed of honorable and courageous men of old and woke up with a start when Barnaby's face emerged among them. Mara rubbed her eyes and stood on shaky limbs. The door to the library opened, and Hirsch announced her guests.

"Mr. and Mrs. Rogers are here to see you, miss."

"Show them in. Please find Mr. Barnaby and request him to join us."

"Miss Mara, should dinner be served in the

library?"

"We shall eat in the dining room."

Hirsch returned moments later leading Barnaby and his guests.

Barnaby cleared his throat. "Miss Mara Highbridge, I would like to introduce Maggie and Graham Rogers to you."

"Welcome to Woodhaven. I am watching it while my sister and brother-in-law are visiting her parents." Mara reached out and shook hands with them. "I am pleased to meet you both. Barnaby told me you are friends from his childhood."

"This house is rather remarkable. I have driven by it many times. Each time I wondered who lived here and what it looked like inside." Maggie smiled and looked around the room. "I know the circumstances are beyond your control. Please know I am only here to help and protect you," Maggie said.

"Miss Highbridge, you will find my Maggie to be a real asset. There is not a better woman protector in all of London."

"Thank you, Mr. Rogers. I am not sure this is necessary." Mara bit her lip and shook her head. "Mr. Barnaby just takes over everything whether I want him to or not."

I cannot believe what I just said. On the other hand, I am actually taking a stand. First time for everything.

"Miss Highbridge, rest assured Barnaby knows what he is about. He has explained what transpired in the last two days. He and I plan to get to the bottom of this problem you are facing. Maggie is going to be here to make sure nothing happens to you, your store manager, and the three lads."

"Yes, but the question is whether this is necessary. Could this not be a case of mistaken identity?"

"We should be able to find out in a reasonable time. Four of my men will be in the estate manager's vacant house before midnight. Their job is to watch over the main house and make sure no harm comes to you or anyone else."

"Come to the fire and warm yourself. I can ring for some drinks or tea. Mrs. Millbe, our excellent cook, is just putting the finishing touches on dinner." Mara could feel her cheeks warming from her lack of manners. She might not be happy with Barnaby, but that was not any reason to take it out on her guests.

The two couples sat for a long time, discussing what had happened late yesterday. There was no doubt Barnaby had saved her life and those of the lads. The discussion always came back to who and why.

"I had all day to think about what happened. Now that we have discussed it at length, there is only one recent incident that I believe can have any bearing on this." She told them about Mrs. Pearly's party late last year and the women discussing her. They thought Mara looked just like the hand-painted portrait brooch of a woman in the French court their cousin had in his possession.

"Since then, I have been attending every social function I can get an invitation to. I had hoped to recognize the women's voices. Unfortunately, I did not see their faces. Their backs were to me. I could not get to their location due to a small garden between us. Trees and bushes blocked off the entrance to a portion of the room I found myself in. When I finally found a path of sorts through the greenery, the women were gone. I tried to find out what I could without drawing attention to myself. I am now waiting for information from my foster mother who raised me from the time I was a few days old."

"Hirsch informed me this afternoon a messenger delivered a package. While I retrieve it, you might want to explain to Maggie and Graham about your foster mother." Barnaby hurried from the room.

"There is not much to explain: Catherine Highbridge recently became the Duchess of Russellton. She is my foster mother and raised me. I believe she may hold the key to the identity of my parents." She puffed out her breath "I have mixed feelings about finding them. Most of the time I would like to know who they are, but a part of me is afraid of what I might find. They could be evil people or—"

Barnaby came back into the room and sat next to Mara. He handed her a package the size of a thick book, wrapped in soft fabric, and tied with green ribbon. They all sat on the edge of their chairs.

"Hirsch just told me he had to sign for it. It came from Hatton Garden in London's Jewelry Row. The delivery man had an armed guard with him."

Mara inspected the package as she placed it on her lap. "I am at a loss for words. Would you please open the parcel?" She held it out to Barnaby. "After all it is addressed to you."

He removed the ribbon from around the paper. An envelope with a wax seal lay across the inside flap of the cloth. Under the wrappings he discovered an ornate wooden box, which Barnaby set down next to his chair. He walked over to the desk to retrieve a letter opener and returned to Mara's side.

She grabbed and opened the envelope with her nail. Taking out the paper she handed it to Barnaby. "You must read it first."

He shook his head and opened the folded paper.

Dearest Barnaby,

I received a most urgent request from Mara. Nicola arrived at Highbridge Manor, and we discussed Mara's actions over the last few months. I have come to the conclusion she should receive all the information I have regarding her birth parents.

I am taking the liberty to request you assist her in the days ahead. I had hoped to discuss this with Mara on my next trip to London. But circumstances beyond my control will be keeping me at the manor until later in the year.

I was handed the enclosed item in the velvet bag immediately upon Mara's arrival and told the contents would cover raising her to adulthood. I kept it safe all these years. I imagine it to be a clue to her birth parents or at least her mother.

Mara must also be aware the woman I believe delivered her to me is The Duchess of Hempwood. She would have all the answers Mara is seeking. I am sorry I cannot be of more help. I am not sure the duchess will see Mara. She is a recluse since her husband died a few years ago in tragic circumstances.

We all send our love.

Catherine

The Duchess of Russellton

Barnaby unfastened the lid to the box and took out a drawstring velvet bag. He offered the item to Mara. "I believe this is yours, my lady."

She stared at the item Barnaby placed in the palm of her hand and shook her head. "I do not want to open or touch it."

"I distinctly remember you telling me you wanted to know who your parents are?"

"Yes, I heard you say so, too, just moments ago." Graham stretched out his legs.

"I do one moment, and then the next, I don't care. Remember, my parents gave me away. I am so confused." Mara looked at the floor.

"At least look into the bag and see what is there." Maggie walked over and patted her arm to get her attention.

Graham jumped up and added some coal to the fire and stood with his back to the welcoming heat.

"I will be happy to assist you in your search because I have a better understanding of your story." Barnaby did not wait for an answer. He grasped the bag and poured the contents into his left hand. In his palm sat a stunning teardrop diamond on a braided silver necklace so elegant it looked like a single strand of thread.

Maggie hurried over. "Might I see Mara's prize?"

Barnaby handed it to her.

"I don't believe I have seen a piece of jewelry so perfect or beautiful. It surpasses the diamonds in the crown jewels in the London Tower. I wonder where it came from?" Maggie passed it to Mara.

"What could this mean? The value must be enormous. I…it is not something I can wear in public. Do you think I could or should?" Mara picked at her thumbnail.

"No," Maggie almost shouted. "You would be

noticed at once. Something like this would be recognized within seconds and most likely by the wrong people. I realize it could help you discover who your parents are, but not in the way you hope. It would be better to take it slow. Do some investigating before you show it to anyone besides the four of us."

"Would you mind if I examine it?" Graham walked over to stand in front of Mara.

"Please do. I am curious about its value." Mara placed the necklace in Graham's outstretched hand.

He produced a jeweler's loupe from his pocket. He walked over to stand next to the lamp to study the facets of the cut stone.

"Maggie, I appreciate your and Graham's concerns. However, I do not know you. Barnaby just told me you both have been friends for years, and that you grew up together. Please understand, I am a very private person. There are some situations I might not want to talk about or share with anyone I don't know. I..." Mara shook her head, not that anyone noticed.

"I understand what you are thinking and saying." Maggie chuckled. "Let me tell you about Barnaby, Graham, and myself. We grew up together, living on the same street in the East End of London. There are many incidents we took part in we are not proud of. There are some we wish we could share with people. We saved lives with our words and deeds. Graham and I still live on the same street because these people are so much a part of our lives. We help when we can. We feed and care for many misfits.

"In the past, Barnaby saved our lives, we his, and those of our friends more times than we can count. When he went to fight Bonaparte in France, he even came to our rescue there a time or two. He is the brother I never had. I would give my life for Barnaby any day and any time. I pledge never to betray you or your family."

"I cannot add more to Maggie's comment other than that Barnaby is part of our family." Graham crossed his arms over his chest and sat back in his chair. "There have been times I have been furious with him. Our relationship is too old to let anything change who and what we are to each other. Know I will protect you and your family with my life.

"Regarding this necklace—I do not believe, in all my years, I have seen a finer diamond than this." Graham put the necklace in Mara's hand. "You must *not*, I repeat, not wear or show this to anyone outside this room until we discover more about it. It is worth a fortune. An enormous one."

Tears rolled down Mara's face. "I do not know what to say other than I trust Barnaby." She sighed and added, "And both of you." She dried her eyes and sat back down. "I must think this through."

Now is the time for me to make my own decisions and hope they are the right ones.

A hard knock on the library door caused everyone to turn toward the sound.

Chapter Five

The butler walked in and stood just inside the door. "Miss Mara, a man at the kitchen service entrance requests to see Mr. Barnaby."

"Bring him into the library."

Hirsch straightened his posture. "Miss, the man's apparel is not proper for admittance to the library or this house."

"Did the man by chance give a name?" Barnaby stood.

"He did. Samuel Tegor."

Barnaby shrugged his shoulders. Without warning he spun around toward the butler.

Mara looked at Barnaby with eyebrows raised.

"Show Mr. Tegor in," Barnaby said.

"Miss, his clothes are filthy. He smells like the docks." Hirsch wrinkled his nose, grasped his hands behind his back, and rocked heel to toe.

"Escort Mr. Tegor here. Now, Hirsch."

Mara's hand covered her mouth the moment she realized what she'd just said.

I cannot believe I spoke to a servant in such a manner. I have never used that tone of voice with anyone, even my sisters.

She turned away from the retreating butler and stared at Barnaby. She slipped the necklace into her pocket, and then pushed the box and paper under her chair.

"What is so funny, may I ask?"

"His last name."

"I still do not understand."

"You will," Graham said, with a smirk on his face.

The butler shut the door behind him and slowly walked back to the service entrance. He snatched the teacup out of the man's hand.

"Follow me."

Mr. Tegor's clothes were speckled with dirt. Streaks of mud ran around his pant legs. His boot toes were caked with dried mud. His unbuttoned coat revealed a dirty white collar. He wore a thick, dark brown leather belt with a large knife in a scabbard on his left hip. His clean nails were cut short. Numerous cuts and scrapes graced his chaffed face. He did look freshly shaved, which seemed at odds for the time of day. His long hair was secured with a leather string at the nape of his neck. Bushy eyebrows matched his dark brown hair. By the looks of him, he'd led a hard life.

Barnaby recognized him immediately.

"Samuel, I knew it had to be you. The name gave you away. You are a sight to behold, considering I thought I would never see you again." Barnaby hurried across the room and reached for Samuel's outstretched hand. At the last minute, he reached out, hugged his brother, and looked into his eyes. "You have aged."

"You as well. Time stands still for no one. It is wonderful to be standing on English soil once again."

Graham said, "We sure have missed seeing your sorry—

Maggie cleared her throat.

He looked at Mara. "Oh, sorry, miss, I—"

"Not to worry. I am sure it will not be the last time you almost say an unmentionable part of the human body." Mara chuckled.

Maggie reached over and hugged Samuel. "We thought you were lost to us forever."

He patted her on the back. "I am glad to see my favorite people all together in one place."

Barnaby took Mara's hand. "I would like you to meet Miss Mara Highbridge. While the owners are absent, she is the mistress of Woodhaven Estate."

Mara shook Samuel's hand. "Welcome. I know my brother-in-law will be disappointed he is not here to receive you."

"Ladies, if you will excuse us. I do not believe Samuel came just to let us know he is back in England. Am I right?"

"Right on the mark, as usual, little brother." Samuel reached out to Maggie and grasped her hand. "It is an unexpected pleasure to see you."

"You take your hands off my wife."

"Tell me you did not marry this rogue?" Samuel put his arm around her shoulder.

Maggie looked up at him. "I did, and you know," she said, "I am not sorry, either. Mara, you and I have much in common. I think we should retire to the sitting room to discuss Creations and the amazing school you have started."

Mara would much rather have listened to the men's conversation. The women's world she found over the years happened to be full of encompassed fluff and meaningless actions. The gentlemen's world proved filled with far more exciting and challenging events.

"Maggie, would you like to have a drink? Barnaby,

I would have a whiskey. Would you please do us the honors of pouring me one and getting Maggie her choice?"

"I would be honored. Unless Maggie has changed, I am sure she will have the same as you." He looked in Maggie's direction.

"I always knew you were smart. This just proves it," Maggie winked.

He poured an ample amount of the amber liquid in each glass and handed one to Maggie. With the bottle in one hand and two drinks in the other, he walked over to Mara.

With a huge grin, he said, "Here you are, my lady."

Mara took the glass, reached out, and pulled the decanter out of his hand. "We might require more refreshments." She turned and walked out of the room with Maggie right behind her.

The second the door closed behind them, Maggie said, "Mara, well done. I wish you could have seen the look on the men's faces."

"I am sorry if I offended you. I could not resist. Men seem to find the need to tell women what to do. Usually, I say little, but the new me will not tolerate such nonsense." She motioned Maggie over to the fireplace and plopped down in one of the chairs. She sat her drink and the bottle down on the small table.

"I liked you the minute I met you," Maggie said. "Now I know for sure we will become fast friends. I wonder how Graham and Barnaby are going to manage the two of us?"

Both women sipped their drinks and sat lost in their own thoughts for a few moments.

"Mara, tell me about yourself. I can see you are

successful in your business. I have many friends and acquaintances who frequent Creations. But I do not recall anyone mentioning your name in relation to the shop. They discuss how fashionable the clothing is from the foundation garments to the shawls, capes and such. I know a few women who do not purchase from any other dress shop. Believe me, that is very unusual. I own a few"—Maggie raised her eyebrows—"actually more than a few articles of your wonderful clothing."

"The *Ton* would not accept me if they knew I owned a shop. Until coming to stay at Woodhaven on a temporary basis, I lived with my aunt in a unique area of London with my younger sister. We had no idea what our new accommodations would mean to our dear Aunt Belle when she invited us to come and live with her. Shortly after arriving at her home, we discovered she was being shunned by most of London's society.

"Many of her acquaintances stopped coming to see her. We offered to leave and move back to Highbridge Manor, which is in the country. Our dearest aunt refused to listen to such nonsense. We came to London to follow our dreams. She would not hear of us running away.

"I started a small enterprise and hired Susan Summers to be my manager. In truth, we struggled for the first couple of years. I have been meticulous to hide my ownership of Creations and the fact I am the clothing designer."

"But why keep yourself a secret? It is a success. You should enjoy it."

"I have had a problem all my life in that I do not like to be noticed. I am good at planning and managing details but prefer hiding in the background, away from prying eyes. I have accomplished my dream of a fashionable dress shop, and much prefer to stay hidden from view. No one knows who I am in London. I am just another woman in a vast sea of the growing population in the city. And truth be told, I enjoy it. It is my little secret. Until now, I have been willing to let my older sister be my champion. I am not sure why other than it made my life easier. I am always the calm, quiet, reserved sister. All that, I hope, will be changing. I am not certain if I am afraid or not. It is past time I take responsibility for myself, which means fighting my own battles, large or small, and no more hiding from view."

"Bravo for you. It is not easy. I have been Graham's secret partner in every transaction since we became a couple. My name is always kept out of the business dealings, mainly to protect me from the underbelly of London. It is interesting the amount of information I have gathered over the years because people do not see a woman being smart enough or cunning enough to be in business."

"You are a woman after my heart. No one but my older sister ever understood me. She is very independent. She has fought more battles against the male establishment than I could ever hope to. I have always been in the shadows. She was the leader, I the follower when we were all growing up. Nothing ever changed until now."

"Graham mentioned you started a school for anyone who wants to learn to read and write. I ask because, while I can do both, I must admit my favorite subject is mathematics. I do the books for Graham. His interests are many, and he never keeps anything straight. People have learned to come to me for financial matters, but many do not like it. I would like to be part of your fantastic project to help and improve the lives of people in the East End."

"There, again, I have remained the unknown element. I hired a woman when the school began. She is a marvel and believes, as I do, every human being in London should have the same rights and privileges, regardless of his or her social standing. I supply the money for the school, but I do not take part in any of the planning. Creations is the sponsor—nothing more, nothing less. So once again I am concealed far in the background, just the way I liked it, until now.

"Tomorrow I will take you to a building I have purchased next to the school. I call it 'Home Sweet Home' in my mind's eye. At first, I planned to enlarge the school, but now my intention for the structure is changing. When it is completely renovated, it will be a place for those without homes to live in while they receive the training for a profession to help them secure an honest living—one they can be proud of.

"I am determined to take charge, let all London know who I am, and what I am about. I shudder to think about it. Yet I am determined. I know I probably should take little steps to begin, but there is no time. So, I shall jump right into the fray and do the best I can. I would consider it an honor if you were a part of this undertaking."

"I would love to be a part of such a grand plan."

"So you shall. We can make a difference in London. Did you know people have gone missing, especially young children, most often girls? The rumor is the girls are being taken to other countries and sold as sex slaves and boys as work slaves. I hope to find out more about this and work hard to put a stop to it. Our young citizens deserve better."

The women talked for hours and formed a friendship that if Mara had not been attacked would otherwise not have happened. In fact, they most likely would never have met.

The entire time the women talked both of them wondered what the men were discussing. It seemed they always got left out of the more exciting conversations. Or did they?

Chapter Six

When the ladies secured the library door, Barnaby rang the bell pull and requested the butler bring another bottle of whiskey. Hirsch poured the gentlemen their drinks and left the bottle on the table.

"You know what the authorities will do when they discover you in London?" Barnaby sat on a chair directly across from his brother. "It is not so long ago since you were transported. Many involved in your case are still in positions of authority."

"Put an end to your anxious thoughts of my being caught and hanged. I have been cleared of the crime. The worst chapter of my life is over and thankfully done with." Samuel tipped his head back for a moment and closed his eyes. "I know you tried your best at the time to prove my innocence. Thinking about and discussing them days makes me glad I am still alive.

"I have a letter from the Australian government proving I had no part in the dandy's murder." Samuel stood to walk off his nervousness. "A man transported two years after me confessed to the authorities after I saved his life and his family."

Barnaby passed the whiskey bottle around. When it came back to him, he set it on the side table. "Help yourselves. If you would like something else, Hirsch will procure it."

"If I drink much more I will not be able to go

anywhere tonight. I do have my business rounds to make." Graham held up his glass. "You would be amazed at the information on the street late in the evening, or I should say early in the morning. Especially after people have consumed a fair amount of spirits." He took a sip. "Cannot drink like I once did."

"So, brother, what brought you back to dear old London?"

"Sex trafficking."

"All the way from Australia." Barnaby frowned. He crossed his arms over his chest. "You are serious."

"I must go back to the beginning to make sense." Samuel paced around the room, stopping from time to time as he spoke. "I took the only honest work I knew working on the docks although many were falling down. You should have seen them on a rain-soaked night: uneven boards were ready to trip anyone walking along. Some were even missing, and others were so loose that if you stepped on them wrong, your legs would be dangling into space with the water lapping at your toes." He grabbed the back of a vacant chair and leaned against it. "One man hung suspended for hours until someone came along and rescued him. Part of the dock sat so lopsidedly it was hard to walk when a strong wind came up. A few men even dropped like stones into the water never to be seen again." He held his empty glass to his lips, then laughed because it was empty. "The docks were much worse than the ones I left in London, behind the warehouse. Remember those?" He poured some spirits into his glass.

"How could I forget? I almost lost my life one night when I fell into the Thames." Graham shook his head. "I have hated bodies of water ever since."

Samuel took a sip from his glass, took a deep breath and continued. "Once many of the thieves and cutthroats landed in Botany Bay, they continued to ply their trade. Some found a return trip to England hiring on as crew members. Nothing changed for them, except the location of the dastardly deeds they performed." Samuel set his glass on the nearest table and rubbed his hands together. "There was some honest folk from the debtors' prison, trying to survive in a land with lifetime criminals. I finally found a group of men and women willing to regain their self-respect through hard work and honest living. It did not take long for the government authorities to notice, for when we worked, nothing went missing." Samuel rubbed at his nose. "Many in the government posts were as bad, if not worse than, the criminals. My friends learned to stay clear of such people, and we defended our principles when necessary. We established ourselves, men and women alike, with the government and local citizens too. We kept the riffraff out of our operations and in time made a decent living. The undesirables stayed away. It did not take long for them to know we would either turn them over to the authorities or make them vanish. In the last five years, I've expanded my operation to include trade and export of local products."

Samuel stopped to take a breath and emptied his glass. "Actually, my company has done right well for itself. About two years ago, my friends and I discovered, or I should say we noticed, some ships coming into port never came to the docks we managed. They laid anchor in the harbor, sometimes for days, until one of the dishonest wharves was open to receive them." Samuel sat in a chair near the fire. "It did not take long to figure out they did not want us to see who or what they were bringing into the bay. About the same time, the government hired us to do some investigating, which we did, and which is my reason for coming here about a year ago." He set his glass on the table.

"You mean to tell me you have been in London all this time and have not contacted me? Why?"

"Brother, you of all people should be aware things are not always what they seem. To keep up my pretense of not knowing anyone in London I could not be seen with a toff and titled friend to boot. I would never have got any of the information I came for. The main reason I am here is to find the slave traders who are sending, for the most part, English children to Australia and other countries to be slaves." Samuel stared down at his hands. "For girls, it is to be sex slaves. Believe me, it is not a pleasant sight." He shook his head. "I have seen it first hand and have been working on the docks watching and waiting for the next shipment because London is the starting point. I have come to ask for your help."

"Brother, how can you be sure the city is the starting point?"

"I'm not surprised," Graham said. "But I've never had the opportunity to discuss this with any honest person."

"It's straightforward once you understand the history. When my dock mates and I discovered what cargo was being unloaded, we followed the children and rescued the lot. There were twenty girls aged eight to thirteen and all English." He leaned forward in his chair. "Their ship initially sailed from England. Fifteen were from farming communities in England and had not been in London for long. According to the young girls, the rest came from coastal ports on the way to Botany Bay. Ten children had been dropped in other ports during the journey. Their sexual training started on the ship. They either did what they were told or were thrown overboard. The second day out of port a brother and sister were thrown overboard because the children refused to put on a sexual show for the crew." Samuel clenched and unclenched his fists. "The remaining children were made to watch them drown. Some of the girls still hear their screams in their dreams. From then on everyone did what they were told."

"My father, rest his blackened soul, always said crimes against children were created by the evilest of men on the face of the earth." Graham shook his head. "It is the only criminal activity my father never took part in."

"Samuel, how long"—Barnaby pounded his fist on the arm of the chair with every word he spoke—"do you think this slavery has been going on?" He stood up so he could walk off his anger.

"I would wager since ships have been sailing. Sex is a lucrative trade. How many establishments are right here in London? And I bet you can discover sex slaves right here under your very noses. If a girl loses her parents, and there are no siblings or other family members, how will she feed and clothe herself? Many have no choice." Samuel took a deep breath.

"Do you remember when we were about ten or twelve and we heard screams and followed the sounds to the docks?" Graham shook his head.

"Yes, and I shall never forget the huge man

jumping out from behind the warehouse and warning us to vanish like the wind, or we would end up on the ship." Samuel rubbed the back of his neck.

"I must not have been with you—"

"You were home with our mother that night and madder than hell because you missed all the excitement. We went back the next evening, and the ship had left port. We never saw the big man on the docks, and come to think of it, the ship either." Samuel leaned back in his chair.

"I think you will find the following information more than interesting. A drunken worker on the dock blabbed a story to me less than a week ago. Said he had a chance to earn a great deal of extra cash. All he had to do was snatch a woman off the street for £200. He was to meet a man at the Red Rooster Inn for more details. He passed out from the drink before he could meet up with the man and had not been able to find the contact person since."

Barnaby sat back down in his chair and leaned forward. "Do you know the woman's name?"

Samuel shook his head "Not then, I didn't. However, two days ago I ran into the same sailor. Once again, he could hardly stand upright. I quizzed him about the woman's name for the price of a drink. Once he got his swill, he told me it was a Miss Mara Highbridge. I wanted to question him more. He passed out. I have been watching you, brother, from afar. I finally put two and two together and realized she is your Miss Highbridge."

"My—What made you say my Miss Highbridge?"

"The look on your face every time she is close to you. You may think no one notices. Little brother, you give yourself away."

Graham snickered out loud. "I would not call him little. He is about four inches taller than your six feet. Not only is he taller but bigger than you overall. Come to think of it, you were the smallest of your family."

"I only call him little because he is the youngest of us. I sometimes wonder how we ever survived?"

Barnaby tapped his foot on the floor. "Did your mate say what the man wanted my Mara for?"

"No. I listen to the chinwag on the docks. Something to do with expensive jewelry from France, stolen shortly before or during the Revolution."

"You, brother, are a bundle of sad and depressing information." Not waiting for a reply, Barnaby asked, "Do you have a decent place to stay?"

"No, just a room near the docks." His hand automatically touched the scabbard on his belt. "No one bothers me since I established I can fight and handle a knife."

"Since the recent kidnapping attempt on Mara, I have been staying at Woodhaven as added protection for her safety. I have rooms not far from the docks but distant enough. There is no worry about the thugs and thieves who thrive near the Thames. I would be happy to show you my rooms in the boarding house and let you stay there while I am at Woodhaven."

"I would appreciate it, more than you know. I don't think I have slept soundly since my arrival."

"Let's go and get you settled in. I would like to check out the docks. The government had concerns not long ago. There has been stealing from the warehouses and missing dockworkers. I have been gathering information. So far I've come up empty-handed."

"The women will be safe while we are gone?" Samuel stood.

"Yes. Graham's friends are on the premises to protect everyone in the house."

"And to set your minds at ease, Maggie is the same now as all those years ago. She has not changed a bit. She can still handle herself. Besides, I taught her all the tricks I know."

Graham strolled out of the library to confirm his men were in place. When he returned, the three friends left through the side door. They rushed to the front of the house and down the street. In no time they found a hansom cab to take them within a few blocks of the docks. The men approached Samuel's boarding house on foot, gathered up the few items in his room, and were gone before anyone noticed.

"By the looks of your possessions, you are not planning on being here long." Barnaby pointed to the small bag his brother held.

"I learned long ago if you do not have anything worth stealing, no one bothers you. It is much safer this way, believe me." Samuel slapped his brother on the back.

They strolled to Barnaby's lodging which consisted of the entire top floor of a three-story house. Barnaby had never figured out his landlord's age, only the fact he'd spent most of his life at sea. He unlocked the front door, walked over to the first door on the left, and knocked numerous times. Samuel and Graham stood back at the entrance to the house. A stooped old man opened the door and hobbled into the hallway.

"Mr. Marc, I would like to introduce you to an old friend from the East End and my brother." The men shook hands. "Samuel needs a place to stay. I am at the Woodhaven Estate while my business partner is out of town. Would it be possible for him to stay in my lodgings?"

The man frowned, looking intently at Samuel. "Have him come into my sitting room. I would ask a few questions. You two"—he looked at Barnaby and Graham—"you both be staying here." Mr. Marc opened the door and motioned for Samuel to follow him.

Barnaby leaned against the inside wall and looked intently at Graham. "I hope we are not becoming involved in more than we can handle. What is your take on this?"

"I believe we won't know until we either succeed or fail. Those are the only two options available. Old friend, we can't go back, only forward." Graham grinned. "Guess we shall have to wait and see. It is a game I haven't played in a long, long time."

"Spoken like the true adventurer I know." Barnaby couldn't help but smile. "Just like old times. Let the games begin…"

"I do have a question for you. What do you know about your landlord? He looks old, but looks can be deceiving. I should know. I am in the business of deception. I wonder how he got his money. This place didn't come cheap." Graham looked around the hallway.

"I believe Mr. Marc's former occupation happened to be as a successful pirate."

"Whatever gave you such an idea?" Graham started to yawn. He was getting tired and quickly stretched his arms to the wall in front of him to stay awake.

"The only time I was ever allowed in his sitting

room, I noticed a sword leaning against the wall. The sword is still there in the scabbard. A closer look confirmed my suspicions. It is a Corsair cutlass, and the handguard is solid. The end of the weapon is made like a scimitar and is what initially caught my eye. It's the type used by the pirates in the battle off Cape Gaeta in 1815."

"Is this a history lesson?" Graham rolled his shoulders.

"No. However, you need to be aware of those around you, especially this close to the docks. There are always people departing, many not by choice." Barnaby moved away from the wall.

Graham started to say something when the door opened. Mr. Marc and Samuel walked out.

"Iffin' Samuel pays his rent on time, he can be staying here. No women, no children, and no drinking."

"I can pay his rent." Barnaby took his keys from his pocket to give to Samuel when Mr. Marc stopped him.

"I have another set right here." He pulled a large set of keys from his pocket, removing two. "This one be for the front door, which must always be locked to keep out the riffraff. This here be for your rooms upstairs." He handed them to Samuel.

Barnaby led the way. Samuel and Graham followed him. After he opened the door, Barnaby motioned the men into a small foyer. There were three rooms: a bedroom, a sitting room, and a tiny kitchen. A large, oversized desk sat in the corner of the sitting room. Barnaby filled a carpet bag with his personal items and placed it at the front entrance while Samuel looked around. The men decided to go to the pub on the corner to discuss the mysteries of the man seeking to harm Mara.

There was no doubt in the men's minds there still could be a person or persons trying to hire a new thug to accomplish their goal. Samuel would contact Barnaby when he had something worth reporting.

Once they were seated at a small table, Graham cleared his throat. "Samuel, I am curious. What did Mr. Marc want to talk to you about?"

"He took both of my hands, looked carefully at the tops of them, then turned them over, and looked at my palms. When I asked him why, he said, 'If you be an honest laborer, I got no problem with you being here. Your hands tell me you are not afraid of hard work. You do not look much like you be a hard drinker. This here be a quiet house. I have plans to keep it peaceful. Make no mistake, I can and do enforce me rules.' "

The men parted at the corner. Samuel went to the boarding house. By the time Barnaby and Graham arrived back at Woodhaven, the women were in bed.

The butler met the men in the foyer.

"I owe you an apology for not being respectful to both of you, including Mr. Samuel. I were carried away with my new position, thinking I be better than I be. Miss Mara informed me if you request her to do so she will dismiss me immediately."

"Hirsch, Mr. Graham will be leaving soon. Then I will be off to bed. Make sure everything is locked up right and tight. Tomorrow is another day. You may retire."

"Thank you, sirs." He hurried down the hallway.

Barnaby motioned Graham into the library. "I am thirsty after our walk back to Woodhaven. Why do I get the feeling my quiet life is at a sudden end? Between Mara and now Samuel, I will be kept occupied. I hope you are still willing to assist me."

"Brotherhood forever, isn't that what we pledged so many years ago? Each turn of my life seems to keep bringing me full circle. We are back at the beginning instead of closer to the end." Graham yawned. "I must say all this does keep my life more interesting. It is better to be at the beginning or middle of my life, rather than the end, which will come soon enough."

"We must figure out a way to protect Mara," Barnaby pressed his lips together.

Graham slapped Barnaby on the back and reached for the decanter before his friend did. "One small splash of liquid. Then I am off to see what transpires behind the closed doors of our city. I will see you in the morning.

"We just have to turn over the right rocks to find the sources, which I plan to do this night. My friend, you have been out of this game for a good long time. Tomorrow I will have some tidbits that will be an eye-opener even for you." Graham set the empty glass on the table.

Chapter Seven

A broad smile spread across Mara's face when Barnaby entered the sitting room early the next morning. "According to Maggie, Graham will be here at any moment. How she would know the exact time of his arrival is beyond me."

Maggie entered the opened doorway and announced, "He is a very early riser and demands breakfast immediately."

Graham strolled into the room within seconds of his wife's arrival. "I couldn't find a crust of bread to eat on the way here. I am starved."

"My poor dear." Maggie reached out and patted his arm. "Were you up all night?"

"I did manage some sleep but not enough, believe me." Graham yawned. "I hope there is some coffee."

Mara hurried over and tugged the bell pull. "Breakfast is being served in the library. I believe everything is laid out, except for the hot food." She looped her arm into Maggie's, and they were off, leaving the men to follow.

Once they were sitting at the table waiting for the food to arrive, Mara poured tea for everyone. "Coffee will be coming shortly."

"Might I ask, Mara, what are your plans for the day?" Barnaby reached for his cup.

"I am planning on going to Creations to work on

some fashion plates. Sometime later in the day, I need to see the builders about the building for Home Sweet Home."

"Builders for what? What are you talking about?"

Mara frowned. "I purchased the building next to the school Creations sponsors to make the school larger. Recently I have decided to convert the building into living quarters to accommodate women with children who have nowhere else to go. Now I find I must include children who are on their own in London. Do you know"—she pointed at Barnaby—"children are being taken off the street by thugs and put into…into…"

"Prostitution is the word you are looking for." Maggie pinched her lips together.

"Yes, also trained to be thieves and pickpockets. I—"

"Wait. What did you just say?" Barnaby frowned.

"Were you not listening?" Mara crossed her arms over her chest.

"Yes, but I also happened to be thinking about—"

"Mara, how do you know about the children being taken off the streets?" Graham leaned forward.

"It is common knowledge at the school. It is quite a problem, children begging or stealing whatever they need. You cannot blame a child or anyone for pilfering food. They must eat, or they will die. But the problem is much worse. There is talk about shipping them to other countries. I am not naïve enough to think they would be anxious to go or that they would be offered wonderful homes. I shudder to think what can and will happen to them. I want to train them so they can make a living and support themselves in a proper occupation."

"Who is financing all this?" Graham rubbed the back of his neck.

"Creations, of course. My dress shop is very successful. With my earnings, I pay for the school. I had a delightful home my entire life. I cannot offer aid to everyone, but I vow to support as many people as I can."

"You own Creations? I thought…" Graham looked at Maggie.

"My dear husband, we did not get to talk last night. You made your rounds and then went home. Remember, I stayed here."

"No one but my family and Barnaby is aware of my connections to Creations. I do not interact with customers." Mara folded her hands and placed them neatly in her lap.

"What about the tradespeople? Surely they know who you are?" Graham snatched the pot of coffee off the breakfast tray before Ivy could set it down. He poured himself a cup of the brown, creamy liquid.

"I am a respected businesswoman. The tradespeople I use have no reason to banter my name about as I pay my bills on time, am reliable, and keep my commitments."

"We can talk about this later if necessary. It would be a good idea to write down any information you have on the missing people. Samuel needs to be informed," Barnaby said as he put on his coat.

"Why does Samuel need to know about Home Sweet Home?" Mara raised her eyebrows.

"What he needs to know is why you are proposing such a place. Your reason supports his motivation for his trip to England."

"You know if you had let us attend your meeting in the library last night you could have had this information then. I wish you would stop keeping facts from us. We are smarter than you think." Mara crossed her arms to hide her anger.

"Would you please send the lads with a message to him at the docks to come for our evening meal? We can all discuss this information at that time." Barnaby sauntered out with Graham closely at his heels.

"Did you see the look on the men's faces? I almost laughed out loud. I wonder if they will start including us more in their plans." Mara sighed.

Maggie took another scone. "Do not count on it. After all, they are men and think they must protect us at all times. We have to try and stay a step ahead of them."

The women finished their morning meal and went into the sitting room.

Mara sat on the small couch with a basket of invitations on her lap in front of the fire. "Please explain to me again why you and Graham cannot attend any of the society functions."

"First, we were brought up in the East End, a notorious location in London. Polite society stays away from our part of the city. Many years ago, we both did what we had to do to survive. At times we were not law-abiding citizens. It is not for me to tell you what the men did for a living. I can only tell you about myself."

"You need not say anything. I only care about today and maybe yesterday." Mara squeezed Maggie's hand. "You came at a time when I needed a chaperone and longed for a friend. In my circumstances, I do not make friends easily. I have found one in you. You did not make any judgments about me, and I have made none about you."

"Thank you. There are a few events you must be aware of. I lived a scandalous life. Before I met Graham, Barnaby, and his family, I sold myself to survive. My keeper forced me to steal by giving me a choice of shelter, food, or living on the streets. There are evil and wicked people in this world who prey on girls and women living without some type of protection. I am grateful every day Graham and Barnaby discovered me and took me to Mother Roget when they did. Graham became an honest man, or should I say, honorable as he can ever be, but only after Barnaby forced him. For many years, they did not speak to each other. I am thankful it is in our past. They have since worked hard and long to help people in all walks of life from the East End. Society of today does not let women from my part of London forget for one minute where they belong."

Mara stood, walked over, and grasped the bell pull. Hirsch hurried into the room before she sat down.

"Please bring us some tea and cakes. And please stir up the fire. A cold draft seems to have found a way in here."

Hirsch brought their tea and hurried to put more coal on the fire. "Ladies, is there anything else?"

"Thank you. At the moment we are fine."

The minute the door shut the women giggled while they took a sip of their tea.

"I think I would much rather have had a whiskey." Mara walked over and added some to each cup.

The minute they each took a sip of their refreshed tea they giggled again.

"I think we need to set a timeframe for your search." Maggie raised her hand to stop Mara from speaking. "I wondered if you should take your necklace to Kara's Jewelers here in London and have it appraised. I know them to be honest and discreet. They might be able to tell you its origin. What are your thoughts?"

"I have been thinking, and I must admit not about the necklace. You were forthright with me about your earlier life. It is time to offer some insight into mine. Growing up was a painful time when I was young. The local people in our small town were cruel and mean toward us. Every opportunity they could find, they reminded us we had no family and no parents. They even mentioned a time or two that our families were most likely murderers, thieves or worse. After all, they gave us away. We were unwanted."

"I know we came from very different backgrounds. I can imagine what you went through. Cruel people are everywhere and in every walk of life. Many times, small towns are the worst because everyone knows everyone. There are no secrets."

"My foster mother cut off most ties with the town. She hired tutors to make us worldly by learning literature, music, languages, and history.

"It did not take us long to excel and hone our interests. Mine, of course, was designing clothes. She hired the best clothes designers. They came to Highbridge Manor for a day, weeks, even a month and taught me all they knew. It didn't take long for me to start making all our clothes. Hmm, this tea tastes delicious. I will pour us a fresh cup. People noticed we were in the latest fashion. Cat—as small children we shortened our foster mother's name—made sure we showed off my designs every chance we got. Many times, she was asked where our clothes came from. She told everyone she bought them from a small shop in London called Creations. Imagine our surprise when we heard from Aunt Belle people were scouring London looking for my shop.

"One particular lady always came to visit Cat. None of us paid much attention because she never spoke to us. Actually, she was rude when we were near. To make a long story short, this woman had been trying to locate Creations. On one such visit, she decided to steal one of my design books. I shall never forget Cat and her reaction.

"Shortly after this somewhat unsettling affair, Aunt Belle came and took my younger sister, who had begun to study archeology, and me to London to pursue our dreams. Mine was to actually open my dress shop. Emmy's was to work at the London Museum. Nicola left to practice her herbal skills in a small town. The local Earl's family wouldn't allow their son to marry her because she had no family. Our foster mother made it possible for all of us to have an occupation so we would always be able to support ourselves. I didn't mean to talk so much. I wanted to tell you my story, or at least the highlights."

"I cannot wait to meet the Duchess of Russellton. She is an amazing woman," Maggie said.

"Do you think the men will have discovered anything to aid in our search for some answers?" Mara stood and strolled around the room.

"Both of our men are very resourceful. They know a great many undesirables who usually have some of the best intelligence on any unlawful event. I am sure by morning we will have some new information." Maggie sat back in her chair and finished her tea.

Chapter Eight

Late in the evening, Barnaby and Graham
approached the Woodhaven Estate with caution.
Tonight, they had learned the danger was real and could
prove deadly. It was amazing that a few purchased
whiskeys for the right people got them talking.

At one of the London men's clubs, they discovered
an old French connection. A man who owed his life to
Barnaby and his partner for the help they gave him and
his family during Bonaparte's war in France sat and
talked to them for hours. It appeared many people were
involved with a very expensive necklace. A prostitute, a
con-man, and even a cardinal suddenly became part of
the mystery. Now they would have to gather details to
compare to the facts. Names were needed to confirm
the stories they had heard. However, tonight was still
young. Tomorrow they would formulate a plan of
action.

Barnaby was grateful for Graham's help. He alone
might not have been able to protect his Mara. It had
been years since Barnaby dealt with members of the
East End gang led by Graham. Thank goodness his
friend still had control of them. They had been hired to
protect Mara.

Both men agreed her necklace showed great
promise as the reason for her attempted kidnapping as
they walked from White's establishment. The big

question was how a scandal at the court of Louis XVI in 1785 could involve Mara. It was almost unbelievable.

Barnaby appreciated his friend dealt in diamonds, precious stones, and at one time had been one of the best jewel thieves in all London and even all England. Without him, Barnaby could not tell if a stone was real or fake. The men stopped in the hallway once the outside door was locked and secured.

"I still cannot understand why Mara's mysterious mother sent a diamond worth a king's ransom with her infant daughter," Graham said. "It makes no sense. No one could pawn such a large stone or sell it. It would certainly attract the wrong kind of attention. It could be the reason Catherine Highbridge packed it away. Believe me, my father or any master jewel men back then would not have handled such a diamond. It would have been too dangerous."

"I agree with you." Barnaby grimaced. "That is why our fishing trip, so to speak, today might just reel in what we are looking for."

"More like we were stirring the pot," Graham said. "I do agree from here on out it will prove interesting to see what transpires."

Neither man knew of many people who could afford such a diamond. Both had dropped a few hints. Hopefully, someone would take the bait. They had been careful to imply they were seeking such an article. They made it clear they didn't have it. Had no idea where it could be found. Just that it might be in London. In time, they hoped they could flush out the right individuals.

They were also aware they had just alerted everyone to the possibility some expensive jewelry might show up on the London market sooner than later. The race had begun. From the lonely thief to the expert criminal, they would be tripping over each other to be the first and get the finder's fee offered.

It could prove dangerous for all concerned if they weren't careful. All it would take was to pique the curiosity of one person to start the ball rolling and give them the information they needed to press forward. Tomorrow was another day. They had still to make some crucial decisions. They would smoke their cigars and have drinks in the library as they discussed their options after dinner.

Loud voices greeted them when they strolled further into the back hallway. They knew the ruckus came from the sitting room.

"The young lads were entertaining us with a rendition of two females they saw having fisticuffs in Coventry Garden last night," Hirsch stated. "I don't believe from their description I would call them ladies."

Barnaby raised his eyebrows, and Graham shook his head.

"I wonder what they were doing at such a questionable location and time." Barnaby frowned. "Those three have no sense!"

"Remember us at their age?" Graham shook his head.

"Yes, but we had no one who really cared what we did." Barnaby handed his hat, gloves, and coat to Hirsch. "If we had gone missing, it would have been one or two fewer mouths to feed."

After the butler had taken both men's coats, they strolled into the sitting room. Each stood against one of the opened door jambs. No one observed them for a few minutes. When the lads spotted them, the boys sprinted over and slid to a stop directly in front of them.

"So, the three of you were in the Garden last night?" Barnaby tried his best to hide a smile. "I bet you have a good reason for being there."

"Yes, sir, we does." Jimmy puffed out his chest. "Been following up a lead or two."

Barnaby put his fingers to his lips to silence them. "Let us go to the library and discuss this information."

"After your meeting," Mara said, "would you both escort Susan here? Eel delivered a note to say she would be later than usual—a last-minute fitting for a very demanding client. And Samuel cannot leave the docks. He is planning to see you tomorrow whatever time he can get away."

Mara handed Barnaby the written report she had compiled for his brother about the missing children. It included many names and ages.

"We are going to be eating a little earlier this evening. The lads need to get to bed at a decent time." Mara did not look directly at the boys.

Eel bit his bottom lip. Jimmy and Jeb both shook their heads. Apparently, they had other plans. When Hirsch came back into the sitting room, Barnaby requested the carriage be brought around while they had their meeting with the lads. His new boots hurt, and Barnaby had no desire to walk anywhere.

The boys were to stay at Woodhaven. Barnaby wanted to talk to Susan privately. She needed to be aware of the latest dangers her son and his mates might be facing due to their relationship with the Highbridge and Barber families. Add the new facts of the slavery, and the lads could be at risk in more ways than one.

Hirsch announced the carriage was at the house entrance. The men drove into the mews behind Creations and parked next to the old carriage house.

Barnaby pointed to the open back door when they reached the corner of the shop and started forward. He knew it was always kept locked. He nudged Graham. They entered the building without making a sound and with great care moved to the upstairs rooms using the stairway positioned left of the back door.

Two men sat at the table in the kitchen with their backs to the stairway landing. Susan sat directly across from them. Barnaby put his finger to his lips when Susan saw him. She didn't utter a sound. Barnaby and Graham simultaneously tapped the men on their backs. When they jumped up from their chairs, they were each met with a solid Gentlemen Jim's punch to the chin.

Susan started to cry. "I never been so overjoyed to see anyone in me life. They—" She hiccupped. "They were going to do terrible things"—she swallowed hard—"unless I done told 'em where Miss Mara be." Barnaby handed her a handkerchief. She pressed it to her lips and then moved the damp cloth onto her lap.

Barnaby and Graham took off their belts and used them to secure the men's hands behind their backs. Graham flew down the stairs to the closest pub. He requested someone fetch the Bow Street Runners. Barnaby flipped a gold coin into the air and tossed it to the first man who stood up. Graham rejoined Barnaby. The misfits were sitting up against the outside wall.

"You ain't got no right to keep us 'ere. We ain't done no 'arm," the older man said.

"We be tryin' to get some facts"—he snorted—"be tryin' to quiet her down some. Her be a nervous one she be."

The second man tried to stand and fell back against the wall. "You ain't got no right hittin' us. No right!"

"Susan, I thought the Runner knew he should stay here. Why did he leave?" Barnaby asked.

"Got a note from you. I seen it. The guard had me to read it. I think it still be downstairs."

Susan led the way and found the note in the trash basket outside Mara's office. "I locked the door after he left."

Barnaby read the note out loud.

"We are having a problem at the estate. Come quick.

B.R."

He handed the note to Graham. "Whoever is behind this can write a reasonable message. Damn. Sorry, Miss Susan."

"Not to worry. I have heard worse." She sighed.

"I will stay here and wait for the Runners. I can lock up. You send two of my boys back to watch the shop."

Barnaby was anxious to leave by the time the Runners showed up and took the two intruders to Newgate. Susan locked up the shop. Barnaby and Graham followed after her. They rechecked every entrance and window to make sure the building was secured before they left.

Someone was desperate. Yet the men had not discovered anything that would point to the person or persons behind this. Rather than make Susan describe her ordeal more than once, they told her to wait until they got to Woodhaven. When they arrived, Graham immediately went in search of two of his men and sent them to Creations.

The ladies and the three lads were still in the sitting room, waiting. Mara stood up the minute Susan walked in and hurried over to her. "What happened to you?" She touched Susan's torn dress sleeve.

"Mother, you ain't hurt?" Eel ran over and touched her arm. Tears formed in her eyes. He reached out and hugged her tight.

Maggie rushed over and put her arm around Susan. She led her to a chair in front of the warm fire. "I think we must give her a little bit of room and time. She is safe now and can tell us what happened when she is ready."

Graham walked over with a small glass of amber liquid. "If you drink this, you might feel better." He took a shawl from one of the chairs and draped it over Susan's shoulders. He then moved, sat next to Maggie, and reached for her hand.

No one said a word. Everyone sat looking at Susan. She closed her eyes and took a deep breath. "Sitting with friends it do not seem so—" She sighed. "I must say I was so scared. I 'eard the downstairs door open. Thought it be the lads. They never knock." Susan worried her lip. The room remained silent. She sniffled, coughed, and finally regained her composure. "When them men come into the kitchen I seen it ain't Eel and his mates. They stunk like a privy." She wrinkled her nose. "Before I knew it, they done forced me to sit at the table and started shouting. Asked all kinds of questions about Miss Mara. Where her was, where her be from. They knowed I got a son and be asking over and over where he be. They ain't long with me when Mr. Graham and Mr. Barnaby come in." She smoothed the wrinkles from her skirt and wet her lips. "They going to take me to the boss man, 'cause he paying dearly for info…infor…mation about Miss Mara and family," Susan said. "Thank you both. You saved me from harm." She looked down at her hands in her lap.

Mara walked over and gave Susan a clean, dry handkerchief. "Please do not worry. You are safe."

"Graham and I shall be back after we secure the shop."

"Will you be back in time for the evening meal?" Mara frowned.

"No. We have much to do this night. I do not know how long we will be gone. Do not leave the house for any reason." Barnaby gave Mara a hug. "Four men are watching over the estate. None of you are to leave." He looked at the lads. "That includes the three of you. We do not have time to rescue you or go looking for you."

Before they left, Barnaby changed into his old boots so the men could walk to the shop. This way no one would know they were there. Fixing the door took only a few minutes. Graham's right-hand man and another man from his crew walked around the corner of the building.

"Boss, we just be making our rounds. We ain't been inside. Figured best not to have to explain ourselves to anyone from the magistrate's office."

"Good thinking. Any problem with you two staying the night? You are welcome to go inside." Graham gave the men a bottle each to keep them warm. Barnaby and Graham's men took Jos and Lars on a quick tour of Creations.

Barnaby handed Jos some money. He suggested one of them go and get some food.

"We be finding a place in the building to roost and can stay until either of you show up in the morning," Jos said.

They all shook hands. Barnaby and Graham started the walk back to the estate.

"When I think we might be getting close to having some information, something else comes along."

Barnaby touched Graham's arm. "On the way to the club, I will tell you my plan."

"The toffs have let you join one of their posh clubs?"

"Of course not. I was told when I got blackballed I was not the caliber of the current membership. However, the Earl saw to it I am admitted to any and all. Won't tell me how or what he did, only it was done."

"I had forgotten Clay Barber is the Earl of Woodhaven. Fancy that."

"We have to find a way to keep many of the details we discover away from the lads or they will be in the thick of it. It is going to be hard enough to protect Mara and her shop. Adding the lads to the mix will only stretch our resources," Graham said. "Barnaby, my trusted partner, you have any ideas?"

"We need to use the boys to our advantage. Keep them busy enough, and the lads will stay out of our way. Yes, I have a few ideas." Barnaby looked smug. He turned and walked away. "Wait until I tell you."

Chapter Nine

"Most people ignore children, especially those the age of the lads. The adults carry on their conversations as if they were invisible. The lads listen to everything and miss nothing."

"I am beginning to understand where this is going. Do continue." Graham stuck his hands in his pockets and leaned against the wall.

"We will gather the boys together every morning with their day's instructions, which will be to scurry around the city listening for information. They know where to go and who to talk to. At the end of the day, we will meet again. They can then give us a detailed report of where they have been and what they heard. They can use the Rantipoles street gangs as a source as well.

"Last year the Cato Conspiracy would not have turned out so well without their help. Let's hope this time we all are as successful." Barnaby ran his hands through his hair.

Both men found it easy to convert to their old ways as members of one of the most feared gangs in the East End. Harm one of their friends, then or now, and the people responsible lived to regret it.

First and foremost, the men sought out Samuel to see if he had more information about the slave traders and who wanted to harm Mara. At the docks, all seemed quiet. In fact, they didn't see anyone about. The ships in port looked deserted. No lights shone through any of the portholes. There were no guards, which amazed both men. A few minutes later they went to Samuel's lodgings. Barnaby used his key to the entrance. He had his foot on the first step when Mr. Marc opened his door.

"Good evening to you both. You be looking for Samuel?"

"Yes, sir. Do you happen to know if he is in?" Barnaby unbuttoned his coat.

"How about you both come into my rooms? I want to speak to you." Mr. Marc stood back to let the men enter. Once the men were inside, he walked into the sitting room, leaving the door open. "Something be happening on them docks. I been at sea most of my life. I done seen some terrible deeds I cannot speak of to this day. Sorry things were done to some of the most courageous men and women I ever knowed." Mr. Marc grabbed the arms on his chair until his knuckles turned white. "I still go down to the docks because the ships and sea call me. I do not go iffin' the weather is bad, and never does I venture out much at night. It not be safe. Your Samuel I believe to be in danger. He be followed by some mighty rough men, and they be lookin' for answers. I can protect him in the house, but not on them there docks. You got to warn him. It be best if one of you stayed here with him."

"We cannot stay here. We must protect those at the Woodhaven Estate. I will give you directions and tell the staff to find me immediately if you or someone you send comes to the door."

The old man looked up at Barnaby. "I'll not be

sending you boys on a wild chase. I see we understand each other." Mr. Marc walked the men back to the hallway, closed his door, and locked it.

They mounted the stairs to Samuel's lodgings and knocked. Barnaby was just bringing his hand down to strike again when the door slowly opened.

Samuel motioned the men in and closed the door. "I thought I heard someone downstairs. What took you so long?"

"Your landlord wanted to talk to us and invited us into his rooms. He's very concerned about your safety. I wonder if it could be honor among thieves?" Barnaby looked out the window and then looked at his brother.

"I agree something is going on." Samuel rubbed his hand. "There is no sign of the sailor who wanted to make the quick two hundred quid. I have not been able to locate him. There is no further chinwag about the jewelry. I did talk to some sailors looking for work on ships going to warmer climates. Nothing coming in anytime soon according to the harbormaster. The docks have been too quiet. There are undercurrents like snakes, gathering under a rock, ready to spring out and strike their prey. I have not found the cause. I only know it is there.

"Two nights ago, a new dock worker bought me a few pints just to have someone to talk to. He signed up to be the first mate on a ship coming from Australia and South Africa that would be going back by the same route within days of unloading its cargo in London. For no apparent reason, it bypassed the London docks and went on to Scotland for repairs. His instructions were to wait here. He was told the ship would be returning to London for additional freight and then continue on its way." Samuel slumped in a chair at the table. "He couldn't offer me any information on the type of goods. Just said they gave him money to wait because the freight line is having trouble finding able-bodied seamen. He told me ships always dock in London before going anywhere else. He did not know the current location of the ship, nor its name."

Graham handed Barnaby a piece of paper. "Read this."

"Beware of new men working the docks. Might be the government. The ship plans to be at the dock for only one day. Check everyone out, and if they give you any trouble, kill them. You will be paid double."

"Where did you get this?" Barnaby handed the note back to Graham.

"Last night two men jumped me." Samuel leaned back in his chair. "They threatened my life and said they would only let me go if I told them about my conversation with the sailor. I bashed their heads together, rummaged through their pockets, and found it." He rubbed his hands across his eyes and sat up straight. He took the crumpled piece of paper from Barnaby and sat it on the table after he smoothed out the wrinkles in the paper as best he could.

Barnaby removed Mara's report he had hidden under his shirt and held it out to his brother. "You need to read this. Apparently, Mara is well versed regarding the problems facing the destitute in London. Graham and I think you should find this interesting and helpful."

"Do you think it is wise for you to be working on the docks? Your dubious landlord said he can protect you at the house, but not on the waterfront. I wonder if he has something to do with any of this?" Graham paced back and forth.

"Hell if I know at this point. Anything is possible. I am not sure who to trust. Everyone seems to be hiding something." Samuel scowled as he tried to move about in the chair.

"How bad did you get hurt in the scuffle?" Barnaby suddenly became the protective brother. He walked and stood directly in front of Samuel.

Samuel pulled up his shirt. "Not bad, only a small knife cut. I cleaned it up the best I could."

"You are coming home with us. We can send for one of the healers at the Herbal Center, or Mara can look at it. You can be of no use to anyone if you die. Grab a few things. We will go tell Mr. Marc you're leaving for a couple of days."

"I must be on the docks first thing tomorrow morning. I am so close to this pending disaster." Samuel scratched his head. "I do not want to give myself away. I need and want to solve this once and for all. People depend on me, here and in Botany Bay."

"Do you want to die from an infection or be stuck in bed for days or weeks? You get your wound taken care of now. You can be back at first light. I am not taking no for an answer. Must I remind you we outnumber you?"

Samuel clenched his teeth when Barnaby helped him put his jacket on. The men walked single file to Woodhaven and listened to Samuel grumble the entire way.

Barnaby poured his brother a drink before he went to wake Mara. He knocked and knocked until she stuck her head out the door.

"You'd best have a good reason for waking me."

"My brother is hurt. Can you look at his wound or should I send for one of the healers from the center?"

"Follow me. I helped my sister with her herbal practice until she went to that small town to hide from the world."

They met Hirsch on the stairs.

"Please bring a pot of hot water to the old treatment room at the back of the house behind the kitchen. Ask cook the location of the room if you can't find it."

The butler rushed off while Barnaby followed Mara. The room had not been used much since the Herbal Center opened. However, it was stocked to handle any emergency. After Samuel, with his brother's help, removed his coat, Mara touched Samuel's shoulder.

"Where have you been hurt?"

"Me right side, miss. It didn't hurt much until the walk to Woodhaven." Samuel glared at Barnaby.

Mara gently pulled up his shirt. She examined his festering side and pointed to the table in the corner of the room. "This will not take long. After I remove your shirt, lie on the table on your left side."

She requested Barnaby get one of his shirts for his brother as Samuel's was matted with blood and had been torn beyond repair. While waiting for the boiling water, Mara went to the herb cupboard. She took a deep breath and picked the herbs for infections and healing: rosemary, elderflower, red clover, chamomile, and St. John's wort.

Once the water arrived, she poured most of the liquid into a bowl, added the herbs, and let them steep. Barnaby had earlier made Samuel drink an ample amount of the house's best brandy. She cleaned out the wound and stitched up a six-inch cut. Mara then made an herbal poultice, spread it over the area, and bandaged his side tightly.

"Would you ask Ivy to come to the doorway? I have something for her to do."

Within minutes, the young servant arrived. Mara walked over to her and whispered in her ear. She left and returned with one of Mara's old corsets in her hand. Barnaby and Graham helped Samuel to sit up. She modified the garment with Samuel's knife, placed the corset around his ribs, and secured it.

"Since you insist on returning to the docks in the morning, this garment will protect your wound. It will allow you to breathe easier as your ribs are badly bruised. I can already see the discoloration. Do not be alarmed by the changing colors on your side over the next few days. The color of your bruises will fade as your wounds heal. I will recheck them before you leave in the morning."

The men assisted Samuel to Barnaby's makeshift room where he fell sound asleep the second his head lay on the pillow.

Mara finished cleaning up the room as Barnaby came in.

"I am going back to bed. Your brother has survived to guard the docks another day." Mara touched Barnaby's arm just before she walked out of the room. "I can't wait to see what tomorrow will bring."

Chapter Ten

Barnaby dragged a chair from the corner of the room and sat next to the bed, observing his brother sleep. His mind would not settle down. People continued to jump in and out of his thoughts.

He found himself recalling how, after a close call with the authorities, the Roget family became law-abiding citizens. The moment Mara floated into his mind and his body betrayed him, he got dressed enough to go downstairs. He planned to drink more of his friend's best spirits.

He tiptoed downstairs, being careful to make sure he didn't wake up the others. Without lighting a lamp, he found his way to the library. He opened one of the doors just enough to walk in. Shutting it behind him, he saw the glasses and the decanter on the sideboard. He poured himself an ample drink. If he couldn't get to sleep on his own, maybe the alcohol would help. Tomorrow might prove to be a big day. He wanted to be alert.

He looked over at the fireplace. Someone expertly banked the coals. He sighed.

"Well, do not stand there. Come and sit by the warm fire."

Barnaby whirled around. "Mara? Is that you?"

"Yes. I cannot sleep either. I learned long ago tossing and turning in bed just makes me feel worse.

Bring the whiskey over so I can add more to my glass."

"Would you rather have a sherry?"

"Whiskey is my drink of choice. Are you going to make me get it myself?"

"No, my lady." He opened the cabinet and took out a whiskey bottle. His eyes were by now somewhat adjusted to the darkened room. He topped up her glass.

She slid over to the corner of the loveseat and patted the place next to her. "Please sit here."

Barnaby sat down. "I did not mean to disturb you. If you would rather be alone, I can leave." He set the bottle on the floor between them.

"No, stay. With the number of people in this house, I find the constant chatter many times more than I can bear. I am used to my own company. I have few friends. Yet, when I'm upstairs in my room, I find I do not want to be alone. I truly am scared and apprehensive due to all the turmoil in my life. You know the Highbridge sisters lived a quiet life in the country. Even living here in London, running Creations was a rather dull affair until I started attending social functions. There are times I wish I could go back to my tranquil non-existence." Mara sipped her drink.

"You can never go back. The past is gone and today is right now. Tomorrow is the future and the unknown. If I look back, I find I wonder too much about what could have happened. What if I had done this or done that? Would the outcome have been any different? I realized long ago I cannot change the past. There is no point in reflecting on what is gone forever. I can only impact the present or the future."

"I think I always knew you were not just a common, everyday man. You have much more substance." Mara exhaled. "Perhaps it is why I have always been attracted to you."

"You are attracted to me? Why? I do not have enough of anything to offer you. I certainly do not have a title to provide you with a place in society. I must admit I too, am more than fascinated by you. Mara, I-I care deeply for you."

The couple sat watching the fire for a time. She moved a little closer to Barnaby.

"Would you think me forward if I told you I want you to kiss me?" she whispered.

"You read my mind. I have wanted to do so since the day I first met you." He leaned over and kissed her on the lips.

She put her arms around him and pulled him close. Barnaby continued to hold Mara's hand, "I am not the person you should be thinking of. It is time for me to leave." He jumped up, reached over, and properly kissed Mara. "Sweet lady, good night."

Before she could respond, Barnaby hurried out.

Sunrise was not far off when Samuel faced the outside banister and started to walk sideways down the stairs. He hoped to avoid any that creaked by placing each foot close to the railing of every step. Samuel moved down with great caution, as he needed to leave and get to the docks before anyone would notice him missing. In the process, he failed to see Mara standing with her hands on her hips on the bottom step.

"Where do you think you are going?"

Barnaby moved up behind her. "I believe you have discovered Mara gets up early every day. Would you like breakfast?" He surprised Samuel with a cup of hot coffee. "I believe you still prefer this over tea."

"I do, thank you. I must be getting to the warehouses and the docks. People will notice if I am late. My mission could be in jeopardy." Samuel sipped the hot beverage. "I really must leave."

"You are not going anywhere until I examine your wound. You must come back here when you are finished. Your side needs to be checked after you work a full day." Mara motioned him toward the healing room.

"Brother, you can wipe that smirk off your face," Samuel said through clenched teeth. "I see no point in arguing with her." He turned and followed Mara.

"Have Samuel's food taken to the library. This will only take a few minutes." She opened the door and pointed to the table. "Pull up your shirt. There is no need to take it off." She expertly removed the corset and the poultice. Over the wound, she applied healing salve and a new dressing she had prepared earlier. Mara re-bandaged his side and replaced the corset.

Barnaby came into the room just as Samuel eased himself off the examining table.

"Your food awaits. A hansom cab is at the door. Tell the driver where you want to go. I have taken care of the fare."

After Samuel left, Barnaby and Mara ate. They managed, between bites, to hold hands under the table.

Maggie rushed into the room. "My dear husband arrived a few moments ago. He acquired some new information for us. He couldn't keep his eyes open long enough to tell me. Seems he stayed up all night again. He said he would tell us at our midday meal."

Chapter Eleven

Barnaby departed to take care of some personal business. He vowed to be back no later than one o'clock. If Graham hadn't appeared by then, Barnaby would bring them up-to-date regarding any evening activities he had been involved in.

The house lay quiet after the lads left for school. Susan left for Creations with a bodyguard. Mara and Maggie spent a pleasant morning designing new dresses and capes for evening functions.

Mara took the time to demonstrate how she determined which colors appeared best on a person regardless of their likes or dislikes. More importantly were the person's skin color and hair color. Taking standard pastels, she draped them over Maggie's shoulders. She only did one shade of color at a time.

The lighter, brighter colors made Maggie's complexion radiant, her eyes sparkle, and gave her cheeks a rosy blush. When Mara used dark tones like brown, purple, or green and draped them on Maggie, her cheeks sagged and dark circles formed under her eyes. Maggie suddenly aged. Mara alternated between the spectrum of shades and determined Maggie looked her best in pastels. She could wear others, but it would be necessary to make sure her colors were the ones closest to her skin as they made her look elegant. The cost spent on any article of clothing had nothing to do with how it looked on anyone.

"Mara, what colors are best for you?"

"The shades when the leaves are turning as the weather gets colder: reds, browns, forest-green, and dark yellows."

Mara explained the process of her fashion plates. Both women found the time moved much faster when they were busy. Before they knew it, Graham came into the sitting room demanding food. Mara put away her supplies and walked over to the bell pull. Ivy was prompt, and Mara instructed her to serve the mid-day meal in the library. If Barnaby didn't arrive soon, they would begin without him.

Barnaby turned up just when the trio was sitting down with their luncheon choices.

"Sorry I am late. Contracts with the government are never easy. It seems they always want more than they agreed on. Then they have the nerve to complain when you tell them the cost will increase with their new request."

Graham announced, "I am famished. I did not eat last night. Too busy trying to be in more than one place at a time. Seems I just missed nourishment wherever I went. So, let us eat. Then I can tell you what I discovered."

Mara sighed. "Do we have a choice?"

"No." He shook his head.

Once the dishes and uneaten food were gone, the two couples gathered around the fireplace. Hirsch hurried into the room.

"Will there be anything else, miss?"

"No. We are not to be disturbed this afternoon by anyone. I would like you to make sure the lads do not overhear us."

Hirsch secured the door. Barnaby moved over toward the desk.

"Graham, tell us you have unearthed some good news."

"First, did you bring the necklace and letter from Catherine Highbridge?"

Barnaby took the package from the desk drawer and placed it on the table in front of the chairs before the fireplace. Graham stood and added more coal due to a sudden chill in the room. The ladies draped shawls around their legs.

"I received this late last night. No, come to think of it, the sun had already come up." Graham took a folded piece of paper from his pocket. "A man known to be the most successful smuggler of all time, especially during the Napoleonic War and the French Revolution, presented it to me. He and his crew stole from the French and delivered the cargoes to England by land and sea. The governments were always one step behind him because he had access to many ports. They never found him nor blocked any of his shipments. Rumor on the street is that different countries' agencies, including the English, are still pursuing him."

Graham stood and waved everyone back to the table where they had eaten their meal. "Barnaby, get the lantern." He pointed to one across the room. He fetched another from the desk. He lit the one he held just as Barnaby sat his down. He took the paper, unfolded it, and laid it flat on the end of the table between the lanterns.

"This is a drawing of a very famous, sought-after necklace. In fact, its story is known as 'The Affair of the Diamond Necklace.' A former king of France, not the one recently beheaded, commissioned this necklace for his mistress. Before he could give it to her, the king died. His mistress was banished from the court permanently and never received the necklace, nor did anyone else. It vanished."

Mara proceeded to the desk and opened the center drawer. She rummaged through it until she found a magnifying glass. Bending over the table with her nose close to the drawing, she examined every inch.

"Fascinating. No wonder there were such financial problems in France. This bauble must have cost a fortune."

"Yes, it was estimated to be worth about six million pounds sterling when it was produced. Now it would be worth much more."

"Care to explain why we should have an interest in this French intrigue?" Barnaby rubbed his cheek.

"Open the container Duchess Catherine sent to Mara," Graham said.

"Are you telling me—?" Barnaby pointed to the drawing.

"Just open the gift from Catherine. You never do what I ask," Graham said. "You know, Barnaby, you are a boil in my—"

"Gentlemen, stop right now. I know you like to bait each other. I am not sure this is the time or place." Maggie reached for Mara's hand. "Let me see the magnifying glass. I want to look at something."

By the time Barnaby opened the box. Maggie had laid the glass down.

"Did you not take a look?" Graham reached for Maggie's hand.

"No, but then I know you. I saw the look in your eyes."

"What are you two talking about? I know you are both speaking English but you are not making any sense." Mara frowned.

Barnaby walked over to stand next to her and took her hand.

"Mara, hand your necklace to me," Graham said.

"I would be honored to do so." Mara bowed her head toward Graham. She opened the parcel, removed the velvet bag, and poured the necklace into Graham's opened hand.

He sauntered over and placed the single diamond tear drop next to the one in the drawing and stood back. Everyone moved closer.

"The two look alike. Both are the same size and shape. Can that be?" Mara reached down to touch the sparkling stone.

"Yes, I believe so. In fact, I had considered this before I even got back to Woodhaven. The smuggler told me the story of the necklace but not how he obtained the drawing. Apparently, there is a new interest in the necklace. The smuggler would not offer any information. He had given a blood oath never to reveal his source. He wanted to know if I had ever seen any of the stones."

"Well, have you?" Maggie clicked her nails on the table.

"No. And if I had I would not have forgotten. I believe all the stones are perfectly matched for clarity and color. The little bows at the end of the tassels are rare sapphires. This necklace dates back to about 1785, give or take. It depends on who you ask. It created a massive scandal then, and in some circles, is still considered the on-dit of the day. I told my contact I would begin a search for him. In return, he said he would be in touch with me soon, very soon."

The necklace was returned to the safe hidden behind a family portrait in the sitting room. They knew they were close to the final answer, but something was still missing. They had the what. Now it was time to discover the who. Maybe tonight they would find the missing clues.

Barnaby and Graham left for the gentlemen's clubs to begin their probing for more information.

Chapter Twelve

"I wish we could have gone with them last night and done our own investigating. I dislike sitting here waiting and waiting." Mara tapped her foot on the floor. "I have run out of conversational material."

"What if we went out during the daylight hours?" asked Maggie. "Did you not get invitations to some society functions? Even if we cannot go out at night, surely there are some day soirées we could attend."

"Brilliant idea! Our bodyguards could remain outside while we have our tea." Mara worried her lip. "Let me gather the invitations and see what we have." She handed half of the envelopes to Maggie. They both sat and opened them quickly. "Put any promising ones on the table. Throw the rest on the chair."

By the time they finished their perusal, they had six possible daytime parties to attend.

At breakfast, they would inform the men of their plan and wait for fireworks regarding their idea. The early morning meal came and went with neither of the men in attendance. It seemed they had not returned to Woodhaven the night before. Once the dishes were cleared away, the women went back to discussing their plans.

Mara sent out replies to three daytime functions, two formal tea parties, and one recital for a girl coming out later in the year. Everything sounded tedious but necessary. Hirsch arranged for a carriage to take them to Creations.

"I still do not see how I can acquire new day and evening dresses on such short notice. I know you are marvelous at what you and Susan can do—"

"Everything is under control." Mara raised her eyebrows. "A few months ago, I developed a new way to make clothes. During the season, it is hard to keep up with the demands of our customers. They see a new frock at some function and decide they want one almost identical. Each woman has to look better than the next. They usually come in at the same time and require an entirely new wardrobe. There are a few we started using my new process on before they went to their country homes. Other clients bring in last year's dresses, and we make them anew." Seeing the puzzled look on Maggie's face, Mara said, "A new bow, different lace, or sometimes even a different style sleeve. You would be amazed what we can and have done."

"Dear friend, get to the point. You have me intrigued."

"You are impatient, just like Barnaby." Mara shook her head. "Two months ago, the seamstresses, using the latest fashion plates, many from Paris and Creations, started cutting out very basic dresses from the newest fabric. They used combinations we believe our customers plan to order. Everything is ready to be sewed or is in process. Many are more than half completed. We made sure to have enough accessories to make each dress unique. I believe this can improve sales and delivery of clothing."

"You mean you might have something already made I can wear?" Maggie clapped her hands.

"Not entirely. But what I have will only take a day or two to finish."

"You continue to amaze me. No wonder Barnaby is so interested in you. I hope to meet this Catherine Highbridge. You are a wonder." Maggie hugged Mara. "I am so glad I got to meet you."

Arm in arm, the women walked into the foyer.

****

The days did not drag by as Mara had anticipated. The workers were busy revamping the building next to the school. She spent most days talking to carpenters and bricklayers. People were already camping on the grounds. She tried to figure out ways to keep them at bay. Nothing worked. Mara did her best to ignore them. At night, she could see the cooking fires next to the building and hear the many individual voices. Most seemed happy, and occasionally she heard them singing.

It became necessary to hire guards. It hadn't taken long for thieves and pick-pockets to show their faces, hoping to get something for nothing. During the day it was easy to spot them. They traveled in groups of three or four. Larger groups made too much noise and could be located before they came into view.

Mara found it interesting to watch how the real undesirables operated. First, they looked quite friendly and even offered to do some chores for food or for a place to stay.

It took a week for Mara to stand still long enough to notice what was going on. One afternoon she gathered her nerve and announced they were not welcome. They would have to leave the Home Sweet Home grounds immediately. They all began to move toward her.

The sound of them smacking their doubled-up fists into their open palms sent shivers up and down Mara's spine. Her voice left her when the noise built up momentum and began to bounce off the building. She opened her mouth, but no sound came out. Turning quickly, Mara walked off in a different direction. She tried her best to keep a serene look on her face while her heart raced. Mara knew she wasn't a match for any of the gang members. They all outweighed her, and some were taller than her five feet six inches. When they caught on to her tactics, Mara picked up a three-foot board off the woodpile and carried it wherever she went. She somehow managed to elude them but knew they would be back.

At night she practiced swinging her weapon back and forth in front of her. However, it did not take long for her arms to get tired. Mara finally realized she had run out of options. Mara had made herself a promise she would learn to stand on her own two feet when Home Sweet Home became a reality. She hated to ask for help.

Finally, the Bully Boys, as the lads called them, caught up to her when she stood at the back of the building. They came at her from all sides. Mara wanted to run and hide. She put her hand over her mouth to keep from screaming but found she couldn't move or make a sound.

She saw Eel, Jeb, Jimmy, and the Rantipoles inside the building out of the corner of her eye. Mara watched with relief as they threw open the back door. They all dashed out of the building and somehow maneuvered themselves between her and the gang of thugs.

No words passed between either group. Mara knew the misfits would return in the near future. In the following days the Bully Boys sent in young children as scouts. Mara stood on the third floor of the building. She watched a young boy leave and hurry over to the gang of misfits. Mara was sure these were the same boys who had left earlier in the week. She dashed around the building until she found Maggie.

"I need your advice and immediate help. Let us go and find a cup of tea." They went to the almost-completed kitchen area in the small building behind Home Sweet Home. The cook feeding the workers handed each of them a cup of tea and motioned them over to a small table in the corner.

Mara took a deep breath. "I cannot be in charge of this new endeavor. I have been trying to be more assertive in my life. I can, but only with people like myself. However, the Bully Boys and others like them frighten me. I believe my actions give me away. Hence, I am in way over my abilities and temperament." Mara sighed and put her head in her hands. "I am asking for your help in finding someone who could make this the most amazing place I know it can be. It has to be someone responsible and reliable enough to take on the dishonest, threatening, and mean people who seem to be gathering at the doors. I do not want it to become another disgusting poorhouse."

"Graham and I have been discussing this very thing." Maggie patted Mara's hand. "It did not take us long to notice the gangs and thugs gathering around. There are more than the Bully Boys watching from a distance. Believe it or not, you are the talk of London."

"Why did you not tell me?"

"You have worked so diligently to become more assertive and in charge. I have never seen anyone who is so organized or anyone who has such well-thought-out plans. You are amazing. However, if I had said Home Sweet Home was not the project for you, not only would your feelings have been hurt, I might have put our friendship in jeopardy. In case you have not noticed, I value your friendship. It is the first one I have had since I was a little girl. Real, true friends are not made easily. They do not come along often in one's life. I treasure you. And, in truth, I do not think you would have listened to me. You had to figure this out for yourself and make the right decision, and you did."

"I believe you are right. I just cannot believe I have been so naïve."

"You are not. While your idea has merit, you are right. Someone else would be better suited for handling the evil elements circling your project. Graham and I are willing to take this on if we can be your partners. We can find the right people to work here, ensure they are trustworthy and that they handle their duties with honor. They will have to be paid for their services."

"Of course, they must receive an honest wage. Maggie, you and Graham are the answer to my prayers." Mara sat back in her chair and closed her eyes. "How can I thank you?"

"Thank us? You must be jesting. You are giving people in need the opportunity of a lifetime. It is a privilege to be part of a new era for the working and the poor in London. Graham and I have another great idea for housing. Let us get this off the ground and working properly before we start another project. I see many wonderful plans for you and me in the years to come."

By the end of the next week, Mara and Maggie had the first floor ready for people to spend the night. The furniture, while sparse, was adequate for families. The number in a family determined the area in which they would stay. Most of the living quarters had two bedrooms and a sitting room. Some had a door connecting two units. Large families would be allowed to stay together. Food would be served in a chamber off the kitchen. These rooms were to be a temporary home. There were no cooking areas. The necessary stood behind the buildings. There would be more than one to accommodate the number of people staying at Home Sweet Home. There were shared bathing facilities too.

Large rooms accommodated children without parents, boys in one place and girls in another. Each room would be supervised by an adult. Mara and Maggie spent all day getting the first floor of the building ready for the families who would be spending the night.

Each family or person, child or adult, had to register to stay overnight. If they left after nine in the evening, they could not come back in unless they had special permission. No one would be refused a one-time entrance.

Maggie and Graham hired five people to oversee the operation of the home. It would be run by a committee. Each member would have one vote on any decision that affected the entire facility. The person in charge would change, within the group, on a monthly basis. This would allow each committee member to get a feel for leadership. At the same time, it would prevent one person from running over any of the others. Mara knew it would take time, but it would give the members a chance to learn how to manage the home. The women would participate in the meetings when needed.

In no time Maggie and Graham hired honorable people from the East End to guard the house and the people staying there. In many cases, this was the first decent work some of these people had done in a long time. Graham vouched for those he had chosen. Mara did not worry—well, maybe a little. Many had lived a hard life, and it showed on their faces and in their mannerisms.

They all agreed if Mara saw or heard something she did not like, she could report it to Maggie or Graham. They promised to explain their findings and how the affair had been handled. This way, Mara gained an opportunity to learn and, in the process, would become more assertive.

With everything settled about running the project, Mara decided they all needed to get back to her problem. It seemed everyone had forgotten or at least didn't want to talk about it. Well, enough was enough. Time to move forward. Mara no longer planned to hide behind anyone. Changes would start tomorrow.

Chapter Thirteen

The next morning, Mara and Maggie composed a message and sent the lads to find Barnaby and Graham. Late in the evening, they were enjoying a drink in front of the fireplace when the men came into the house. They heard them because the lads were jabbering nonstop. The women did not move. They just sat waiting.

"We received your message," Barnaby said.

"Why did you feel it necessary to send the lads to find us?" Graham slipped his hands into his trouser pockets.

"Well, we think you are ignoring and avoiding us." Mara looked at Maggie. "It is time to move this nonsense along. I am tired of living like a hermit."

"My dear, there is much you do not understand," Barnaby said. "Explain it to her, Graham. You are the expert."

Graham stopped in his tracks and spun around so he could look at the ladies and Barnaby. "Since when have I become the—?"

"We have been out every night and most of the days obtaining leads and information." Barnaby crossed his arms over his chest.

Graham poured each of them a rather large drink, walked over, and handed Barnaby his. "I think we need to fortify ourselves. I think we may be in trouble by the sound of our ladies."

"Barnaby, would you please be so kind as to get my package from Catherine?" Mara covered her mouth as she started to yawn. "I believe there is some information we have overlooked."

He left to retrieve her package from the safe. He returned within minutes with the box and handed it over.

"Thank you." She opened the container and found the letter. "I do not know what you two have discovered. I believe Catherine mentioned the woman who might have brought me to Highbridge Manor. I want to see if I can contact her and find out what she knows."

"You are right, Mara. However, remember Catherine said the Duchess of Hempwood most likely would not see you. She is a recluse since her husband's sudden death."

"Maggie, tell him what you have discovered in the last few days."

"It took me a while to realize the Duchess of Hempwood will see us."

"What are you saying? We have gone down this path many times in our inquiries with at least a dozen of our contacts. The Duchess of Hempwood doesn't see anyone. We tried everything we could think of to gather information about her." Graham took a sip of his drink, a large one, and started to cough.

Barnaby walked over to the fireplace and reached his hands out to warm them. "No one knows much about her, not even where she came from. We did find out the duchess once lived in France, most likely Paris. Within a year or two of moving to England, she married a duke—a wealthy and powerful one."

Maggie walked over to her husband. "You are probably right about her life before she came to London. However, my mother knew her. They were friends of a sort."

"Your mother was a madam of a high-priced brothel. A very successful one, I must admit, until she fell on hard times. How does that equate with the duchess?"

"She did not always have a title."

Graham cleared his throat. "Are you sure?"

"Yesterday Mara and I went to our home in the East End to get some accessories for the tea party we are soon to attend."

"You and Mara are going to tea? Here in London? You have not said a word to me." Graham stared at his wife.

"And when would I have had this conversation with you? I haven't seen you for days."

"True. Finish your story."

"Back in those days, her name was Brigit Lamont. I remember her teaching me to read and write. She lived with us for a time. She was stunning. I remember my mother saying she had become the men's first choice. And then, one day, she left. However, for my birthday the same year, I received a beautiful bracelet. When I went home with Mara, I found the card which accompanied her gift. I had tucked the note away in my keepsake box. When my mother had no money for food or coal, she had to sell my bracelet."

"Well, I'll be damned. Sorry, ladies. What a surprise. My wife might just get us what we need to figure this all out." Graham walked over, sat next to

Maggie, and kissed her cheek. "Well done."

"Maggie and I have talked this over. We, the four of us, are going to the duchess's home to present ourselves. So be prepared to leave in two days."

"Wait, we cannot leave. Samuel may need us or—" Barnaby said.

"Then we plan to leave without you. The Hempwood estate is not far. We can go in the morning and most likely be home by early evening." Mara went to the decanter and poured herself a drink.

"Do you not think you should wait?"

"For what, might I ask? And no, I am tired of waiting."

"Graham, can you not forbid your wife to go on this possible wild goose chase?"

"Me? Stop Maggie from doing something she wants? You are jesting. Aren't you?" Graham laughed. "Is your memory so short?"

"No, my mind is working just fine, thank you. How can I forget all the trouble Maggie got us into time and time again? We were always watching out for her."

Pounding on the front door of the house stopped their conversation. They heard loud voices but could not understand what was being said. Mara threw open the library door just as Hirsch reached the foyer. The minute he unlocked the entrance, Eel, Jimmy, and Jeb tumbled in. They were breathing so hard, they bent over and rested their outstretched arms on their bended knees as they gasped in shallow, labored breaths.

Chapter Fourteen

Between gulps of air, Eel tried to speak in a normal tone. He could only whisper. "They got her. We got to stop them."

Mara kneeled down in front of Eel. "Who is who? Slow down and take your time."

"Oh miss...we got no time...we got to 'urry," Jimmy said, as he struggled with his labored breathing.

The men herded the boys into the library. Barnaby motioned them to sit in the chairs by the fire.

"Now, who do 'they' have and who are 'they'?" Mara looked at Maggie. "Did I say that right?"

"Yes, you did."

"The slavers got Janey Ann," Eel said.

"Who is Janey Ann?" Graham frowned.

"She is a dear friend of the boys. And why are the three of you out so late? After you had located Mr. Barnaby and Mr. Graham, you were supposed to come back here. It is almost time for you all to be upstairs sound asleep." Mara looked directly at Eel.

"The slave people. We"—he pointed to Jimmy and Jeb—"knowed something be wrong. Them streets have been much too quiet all week. So we snuck out, 'eard screaming and shouting."

"Awful noises." Jeb covered his ears.

"We followed the sounds. Seen them dragging people into an iron cage with wheels two blocks over."

Jeb moved closer to his friends. Tears ran down his face.

"We ain't able to 'elp them," Jimmy said. "We be only three. There be lots of big, mean men using whips and clubs. W-we comes 'ere."

"You must help us." Eel stood.

"Of course we will help you and your friends." Mara patted Eel's arm.

Barnaby called to the butler. "Hirsch, I will give you an address. You must leave immediately. Inform the government man what is happening. He must bring other agents to assist us."

Barnaby and Graham left the room. They returned with their jackets and weapons.

The butler and the carriage driver, Wills, had to wait.

Hirsch held out paper and a pen toward Barnaby. "Might I be suggesting you put your instructions in writing. Otherwise, the government man might not take us seriously. He could refuse to help. After all, we are servants and unknown to him."

Wills handed Barnaby a bottle of ink. He sat down at the desk to write out the message.

The servants immediately left. The men, after a little discussion with the lads, decided it would be best to walk rather than take a carriage or horse. They would blend into the darkness if they were on foot. By now three of the men staying in the gardener's house arrived. Hirsch had sent the kitchen maid to get them.

"You lads stay with the ladies. Mara's kidnapper is still on the loose. Graham and I need to take the guards with us." They hurried out with the other men following. Jeb closed and locked the door behind them.

Mara took one look at Eel, Jimmy, and Jeb. "You lads can leave. Maggie and I will be safe. Make sure you bring Janey Ann back here with you."

The boys talked amongst themselves for a few seconds.

"Jeb, he be staying." Eel motioned Jimmy out the door.

Mara, Ivy, Mrs. Millbe, Jeb, and the kitchen maid went around the house and made sure each window was locked and secured. Mara brought pistols from the library's bottom desk drawer. She made sure they were loaded. Cook went into the kitchen. She returned with two large butcher knives and one enormous meat cleaver. They all sat in the library with the doors locked.

****

Barnaby, Graham, and the bodyguards hurried down the street. They stayed in the shadows. They could hear carts on the secondary roads. Their iron wheels ground on the cobblestones. The sound ricocheted off the buildings, making the noise appear louder than it actually was.

Occasional screams and shouting drifted and swirled through the air. The men stayed parallel with the clatter of deafeningly angry voices. They remained out of sight and carefully watched to ensure no one sat perched on a building acting as a sentry. Curtains on many of the windows parted to view the goings-on. However, no one came out to investigate. Barnaby sent two men to keep a lookout for anyone who might try to stop them. One of the men got close to the wagon cages to confirm the wagons were loaded with people of all shapes and sizes. Most were children.

Barnaby instructed the men to follow the slavers. He and Graham were going to find Samuel. His brother might know more about the ships moored at the docks. He could identify who was in charge of the midnight raid. They ran to Samuel's lodgings and opened the front door. They were halfway up the stairs when Mr. Marc called out.

"What you be doing here so late? Them slavers be out. Heard the sounds of the wagons leaving the docks. Your brother Samuel been gone a couple of hours. I be worried. Went to the wharf but found no one out and about. Him not being back ain't a good sign."

"The lads who assist us from time to time heard the carts leaving. The traders somehow knew where most of their captives were living or hiding. They started rounding them up as soon as it got dark. We came to get Samuel. We should have known he'd be down at the docks and you would already be aware." Barnaby reached out and opened the front door.

"I be coming with you." Mr. Marc grabbed the front door handle. "It be a long time since I have been in a battle. I still remember how to fight. Let me get me sword."

****

Hirsch and Wills did not have any trouble finding the government man's lodgings. They both knew time was not on the side of Barnaby and Graham. After the servants repeatedly knocked on the front entrance, a servant opened the door and scowled at the two men. Hirsch handed Barnaby's note to him.

"It is urgent. Slave traders be about tonight kidnapping young girls. Barnaby Roget, Graham Rogers, and three of their associates be trying to stop them. They must have some assistance."

"Do come in and wait here." The servant motioned them into a foyer. He ran down a hallway. In a short time, a different man in a dressing gown came into the room, holding the note in his hand.

"Before we go any further, how did you get this paper?"

Hirsch bowed his head and stuck out his chest with pride. "I am the butler at the Woodhaven Estate, home of the Earl and Lady Woodhaven. His business partner, Barnaby Roget, and his brother Samuel have been assisting the English and Australian governments regarding slave traders. Mr. Barnaby requested I deliver this directly to you, sir."

"I am not sure I can get men to the docks in time. We must try our very best. Come to the library. I will write messages for you to deliver. I hope both of you can be trusted."

"I do not believe Mr. Barnaby would have sent either of us here if we were not trustworthy. However, it is your decision."

Hirsch and Wills followed the man into the library. The servants received new messages with instructions to deliver them to the addresses on the envelopes. The men hurried to complete their tasks. Then they headed back to the Woodhaven Estate.

Jeb opened the door only after Hirsch and Wills knocked numerous times. Hirsch nodded at the artillery standing behind the young man. He found the various weapons and the people holding them to be a most interesting sight.

"I do not think Mr. Barnaby or Mr. Graham needed to worry about leaving you here alone. Miss, my congratulations on your fortitude."

"Please have a drink of your choice for your efforts this evening. I am proud of both of you." The butler poured two shots of brandy for himself and Wills. Once finished, the men turned to step out of the room.

"Wait," Mara said. "There will be fighting at the docks. Someone must see to the wounded. I am not as proficient as my sister, but I am better than no one." She paused and looked directly at both men.

"Yes, miss, I can guarantee that is correct," Hirsch said. "But I do not think you should—"

"I am not asking your permission. Thank you for your concern. I can promise you this: I have seen many people after they have been shot or injured. I helped her ladyship for many years when needed. You can either come with us,or you can stay here. It is your choice."

"Miss, we shall be coming with you. After all, you may need some protection. Your kidnapper is still out and about." Hirsch bowed his head to Mara.

Wills cleared his throat. "Miss, it might be best for you ladies to dress like gents. What I mean is, that way no one knows who you be."

"Excellent idea. Maggie, we must hurry and change." Mara turned toward the hallway which led to the herbal healing room. "Both of you get the carriage ready. I must gather some supplies. We will meet you at the front entrance." Mara stopped and looked at Mrs. Millbe. "I would like you to put hot water in any type of container you can find because I may need it. I am not sure what time we may return. If possible, I would like to have a hot meal of some sort then."

"Yes, miss. Be careful." Cook turned and left with the maid right behind her.

Chapter Fifteen

Barnaby did not see any activity on the docks. In fact, the entire area appeared deserted. One of the ships did have light shining through a few portholes. The other piers and vessels were barely visible against the night sky. To get closer, everyone would have to hide behind the warehouses. The men continued to watch for lookouts, incoming traffic, or people who should not be out at this hour. Once the coast was clear, they hurried in single file to the next place of cover. A dock guard strolled past them once. It took them almost twenty minutes to go less than one-quarter mile. The closer they got to the edge of the last warehouse, the louder the sound of the carts echoed. Barnaby and Graham had no idea where the remaining bodyguards and Mr. Marc were. It became increasingly harder and harder to tell friend from foe. The men decided they would treat everyone the same until they knew for sure who was on their side.

"Graham, you are aware some of your friends or associates could be involved."

"If any of them are, I promised to be the first to see they get what is coming to them. There can be no reason to treat innocent people, especially children, like this."

"If we get close enough, I believe the traders might give themselves away by their clothes and their smell.

They are indeed a worthless group of men."

"I hope you are right. We do not want to hurt innocent people. We must take it slow," Graham said.

The men discussed the best plan of action. They would attack the carts before they got to the docks to prevent people from the ship helping the traders.

Usually, a ship's crew received a portion of any profits after expenses from any illegal cargo. It was in their best interest to help the traders.

Eel and Jimmy showed up just when they were ready to move into their positions.

Barnaby grabbed Eel by the arm. "I thought I told you to stay with the women."

"You did. Miss Mara and Miss Maggie said we should come and help you. Jeb stayed."

"You best hope your mate is up to the challenge and nothing happens to either of the women," Barnaby growled. He made sure his face did not show he was not surprised they were here. He knew the women would send the lads. He was amazed all three were not standing in front of him.

The carts and wagons crept along at a slow pace. Once they were even with the first warehouse. Barnaby and Graham, along with their other men, shouted in unison, "Halt where you are."

The vehicles ground to a stop. The horses protested. They started to throw their heads, stomp their hooves, and nip at each other. The men driving jumped down with cutlasses in hand and other weapons at the ready. The captives screamed and added to the din of the animals who were now thrashing about. The sudden stop rocked the carts from side to side. The horses sidestepped, pulling the wagons with them. Barnaby and Graham stayed out of sight. They drew their pistols.

The slavers milled around the carts. They tried to calm the horses as they called out, "Who be there? Where you be?"

The captives continued to scream and cry out for help. In the meantime, Eel went to the back of the carts. He picked the locks and opened the doors. Jimmy directed the people who jumped down to run inside the warehouses for protection. When the drivers saw the prisoners fleeing, they scurried after them. Barnaby, Graham, and their men pounced on the traders and guards. Out of the darkness, the government men surfaced. In short order, the slavers were made to kneel against one of the side warehouse walls.

The men quickly crept along the dock to the only ship with a gangway down for boarding. The rest of the moored vessels remained dark and deserted. The water lapped at the dock. The sound masked the noise of their boots creeping up the wooden structure. Barnaby rambled onto the main deck. He turned toward the bridge.

Two crew members rounded the corner. "Intruder, intruder."

The ship filled with a myriad of sailors coming from all directions. Men from behind Barnaby spilled onto the main deck. The scrimmage lasted less than ten minutes. Government agents rounded up the crew. With the assistance of Bow Street Runners, they marched them to join the other captured men next to one of the numerous warehouses.

Barnaby and Graham searched the vessel, looking for Samuel.

"There is only one place where I think they would have put him." Barnaby tapped Graham on his shoulder.

Each man took a lantern, went to the darkened hole of the ship, and found him.

"What made you want to look here?" Graham rolled his shoulders.

"Where would you put someone you did not want to get away or anyone to find?" Barnaby pointed to the cargo hold. "I bet that is where they would have put the slaves too. Such an awful place would stop them from escaping, especially in any port. The crew would have total control."

With the support of a group of honest sailors from one of the other ships, they rigged up rope pulleys and hauled Samuel up onto the main deck. By the looks of him, he'd been beaten until his body was one complete bruise.

"About time you got here," he said before losing consciousness.

Checking Samuel's wounds, Barnaby found a deep knife cut near his shoulder. Someone handed him a blanket. He covered his brother, whose skin felt cold to the touch. He laid his jacket over him as did two other sailors from another ship in the harbor.

"We be getting new coats from the traders," one of the men announced, hurrying away. "They be better-looking than our old ones."

"We need a carriage so we can take my brother and Janey Ann to Woodhaven." Barnaby looked around. Four government men walked toward him with a stretcher.

He heard the sound of an approaching coach. He

should have been angry when Mara, Maggie, Jeb, Hirsch, and Wills exited.

Graham found a dockworker to open one of the massive warehouses. This would allow Mara and Samuel shelter from the wind. The slave traders still knelt in a straight line against the outside wall of the building. The former captives all crowded into the warehouse for warmth. The government men made sure no one approached the prisoners.

****

What awaited them was anyone's guess. Mara hoped she was not leading them into harm's way. But she would never forgive herself if she did not offer aid, no matter how small. After all, someone could get hurt. She just knew she could not stay at Woodhaven wringing her hands and worrying. After all, her Barnaby would need her help.

"I am not going to ask who decided you should come." He looked directly at Mara. "Samuel is badly hurt. Let us go into the warehouse, where you and the rest of your party can be safe." Barnaby led the way, shaking his head. "All of you could have been injured."

Mara bent down to check Samuel and his wounds. She couldn't find any place on his body where there were not cuts and bruises, which marked almost every inch of his body. The new wound on his shoulder would require stitches. By the look of his shirt, he had lost a lot of blood. Recovery could take a long time.

A young girl with a tear-stained face sat down next to Mara.

"What is your name, young lady?" Mara reached out for a clean cloth.

"Janey Ann." She sighed and scooted closer to

Mara.

"Can you go and find Hirsch for me?"

"Who be that?"

Realizing the young girl had no idea who he was, Mara called out, "Hirsch, where are you?"

He materialized next to her within seconds. "At your service, miss."

"I need some water. There should be some in the carriage."

"I will find it." The butler scurried off and returned in a few minutes.

She took some bandages from her bag and cleaned off Samuel's face. She got him to drink a few sips of water. Then Mara stopped the bleeding from his most serious wounds. When she got back to Woodhaven, with the proper tools, she could stitch up his shoulder and any other cuts.

"Nice to meet you, young lady. Can you sit here with Mr. Samuel? Call me if he needs anything."

"Yes, miss." She sat and took hold of Samuel's hand. "I take care of him."

Mara felt Barnaby watching her. There could be no doubt he was furious with her. Did he notice she was looking at him? She sighed. He was everything she needed. Why had she never noticed his crooked nose? She wondered how he had broken it. He reminded her of a knight of long ago, the kind she always dreamed of.

Did he appreciate the fact the carriage hadn't come down the road until the fighting stopped? Mara would explain to him when there was some private time. She still had a hard time taking a stand. This was not the time to think about it. Maybe later.

She moved among the wounded. It didn't seem anyone other than Samuel had severe injuries. Most had cuts and bruises. Of course, everyone would have to watch for infection. It could and did kill many people. She had brought bandages, healing salves, and anything else she thought would be needed. It took almost three hours to get everyone patched up. She checked Samuel frequently and noticed Janey Ann had not left his side.

Mara gathered up the street people and gave them directions to the Home Sweet Home building.

All the prisoners would be taken to Newgate. They marched down the street with their heads bowed. The ship was cleared of all deckhands. Government guards were left on the slave traders' ship and the dock to make sure it stayed moored in place. Just as they loaded Samuel into the carriage, Barnaby walked up to the door. His anger at Mara had left him. He of all people understood her kindness and caring.

"I know why you came." Barnaby kissed Mara hard and long. "Go home and take care of Samuel. Graham and I will follow. There is much to do tonight. I want to find out who is responsible for trying to enslave our young people."

Mara touched Barnaby's face. "Be careful. Evil is lurking about this night."

Barnaby looked around for Maggie and Graham and found them. "Maggie," he said, "Go with Mara. Do not let her out of your sight." He turned and whispered into Mara's ear.

She leaned back and looked into his eyes. "I love you, too." She hugged him tightly. "Be careful."

Hirsch and Wills, with the help of Barnaby and Graham, somehow got Samuel into the carriage. As

Barnaby and Graham stood and watched the vehicle slowly move down the road, Mr. Marc came up to them. "I have someone you need to question. He can shed some light on these here evil doings. If not, I'll be running him through with my sword. I been waitin' years to get even with this vile man. I will not be denied."

Barnaby and Graham followed Mr. Marc. They walked single file away from the warehouses to a small wooden shack which looked more like an old guard house. A former sailor, by the looks of him, stood by the door. The minute he saw Mr. Marc, Barnaby, and Graham, the old sailor stood a little taller.

"Mac, about time. Someone been sniffin' around lookin' for—" He jerked his head toward the small building.

"Joker, you best be gone. Nice seein' you again. Best if we ain't seen together."

"Right you be, Mac." The two men shook hands, and the man hurried away.

"Are you going to explain about your friend?" Barnaby watched the man vanish into the night.

Mr. Marc shook his head. "We sailed together and saved each other's lives many times. This night be my turn to save him."

"And you brought us here for…?" Graham leaned against the shack.

"You be needin' to know who be behind the current slave trade?" Mr. Marc tapped the door. "Well, one of the men inside be goin' to tell all he knows. Wait until you see who he be."

No one heard Eel walk up behind them with a lantern in his hand. The boy cleared his throat.

"Thought you'd need this." He held it out to Mr. Marc then turned and ran to catch up to the carriage heading for Woodhaven.

The two men opened the shed door. There sat Angell, the Assistant to the Chancellor of the Exchequer, tied to a chair. Mr. Marc moved in behind them, shut and locked the door.

"Iffin', you want to live, you, best tell them all you know. Because if you do not, I be goin' to kill you."

"I did not have a choice. They threatened my life and my family…you do not understand what risks are involved. If I tell you, they will have me killed."

"If you do not talk to us, I be running you through." Mr. Marc pointed the sword at his chest. "I owed you for them actions years go against my ship. You were a traitor then. You be a traitor now. You be responsible for many deaths over the years. You thought I died a time or two like the rest. I fooled you. Time for payback, Mr. Fancy-man."

The man collapsed into himself right before them. He talked for a long time. He gave dates, times, and the people involved. Many of the people did not even live in London, much less in England.

Chapter Sixteen

Mara made Samuel as comfortable as possible. He remained unconscious for the entire ride to the estate. Hirsch rushed ahead to make him a bed in an unused storage room tucked into an alcove next to the healing room at the back of the house. It would have been impossible to take him upstairs to a bedroom.

Although Mara had helped her sister over the years, the sight of blood still made her stomach queasy. Years ago, she had learned to block out the color and the smell by leaning back from the affected area. In her mind, Mara pretended the gash was an article of clothing she needed to mend.

She cleaned the knife wound with warm water and stitched it closed with small, even stitches. Then she made a poultice with freshly steeped herbs and laid it over the wound. Mara retreated to the library to catch her breath. She sat in one of the chairs, closed her eyes in the hopes her stomach would settle down. After a short cat nap, she hurried back to check on Samuel. An oversized lantern on a table pushed into the back corner of the room illuminated the space well enough to allow Mara to see him struggling to sit up.

"What are you trying to do? You are not going anywhere for at least a few days. I am going to gather new dressings and some medicine for you to take. I will be right back. Do not move."

He grabbed her hands. "How can I ever thank you for taking care of me? Without your help, I think I would have died. You have been a godsend to my brother and me. He is a lucky man to have found such a beautiful woman."

"Samuel, you and your brother are part of our family. We are more than happy to assist you. Barnaby is an extraordinary man. We have some obstacles to overcome. I hope with all my heart we can do so. Rest, I will be back in a few minutes." She had started to shut the door behind her when Janey Ann arrived.

"He be the man who helped save me life?"

"Yes. We would never have known about the slave traders if he had not come back to England." Mara looked down. "How did you find your way back here, young lady? I thought you were with the lads?"

Janey Ann moved her foot from side to side. "I snuck away from them."

"Oh, I see." Mara shook her head. "Why don't you keep Samuel company while I get some medicine?" She turned back into the room and announced, "You have a young lady to see you."

Samuel tried to smile when Janey Ann walked into the chamber.

Mara whispered in her ear. "Do not tire him out. I will be right back." She closed the door and hurried to her sister's herbal room.

On the way, Mara quietly went and checked on everyone to make sure they had found a place to rest and sleep. The lads were upstairs with Eel's mother. She was not sure how long Janey Ann had roamed around the house. Later when Mara had more time, she would uncover where the child had been. First, she needed to make sure all the doors and windows were locked.

The men were still not home. In truth, she did not expect them anytime soon. Mara knew Barnaby and Graham would not rest until the people responsible for such dastardly deeds were all behind bars. If these evil men were not permanently stopped, they would just change their methods and strike again.

Mara returned to the storage room and found Samuel and Janey Ann fast asleep. She wanted to move the child so she could change Samuel's dressings. Mara pushed and pulled the threadbare loveseat over to the far side of the bed. In the healing room, she found a couple of blankets. Mara moved the child to the makeshift cot. The young girl snuggled under the covers and never opened her eyes.

Mara proceeded to check on Samuel's wounds. She changed the bandages, and again bathed his face and arms. He managed to wake up long enough to take some medicine to keep infection and pain at bay. She moved a chair next to his bed and covered herself with a thick shawl. She closed her eyes and was dozing in seconds.

****

Just as the sun peeked through the clouds, Barnaby entered the house using the kitchen service door. Graham came behind him. They were met by Hirsch, who, once again, had a gun in his hand.

"Good morning, sirs. The house is quiet. I just finished my rounds." He offered a report as to where everyone in the house had settled for the night. He included Miss Mara and their invited guest, Miss Janey Ann. Barnaby and Graham tiptoed into the storage room to check on the occupants.

Janey Ann woke the minute the door opened. She put her fingers to her lips. "You be quiet. Not wake Mr. Samuel."

Barnaby walked over to his brother's bed. Suddenly a hand came out from under the covers and grabbed his arm with a significant amount of force.

"You may look like hell, big brother, but you seem capable of taking care of yourself. Let loose of my arm." Barnaby wiped his hand across his face. "How are you?"

"I feel like somebody beat me up."

"They did. You also acquired another stab wound."

"It hurts like hell."

"Mr. Samuel, no swearing. Miss Mara not be happy."

"Yes, little miss." Samuel tried not to smile in reaction to the child's stern rebuke.

"I must say, could you be quieter? I am trying to sleep." Mara stood and swayed on her feet.

Barnaby reached out, gathered her around the waist, and picked her up. "You, my dear, are going to bed." He walked out of the room.

"Wait, what about Janey Ann and Samuel? I need—"

Barnaby kissed her. She settled her head on his shoulder and fell sound asleep.

"Graham, find Maggie. She needs to take care of Mara."

"I am right behind you," Maggie said, touching his back. "You lead the way."

Janey Ann stood up and sighed. She got Samuel's attention. "Guess it be time for me to be goin'."

Graham hunkered down and looked into the little girl's green eyes. "No, Miss Janey Ann. You are staying right here."

"You be sure?"

"Yes, my dear little friend," Samuel said. "You are not going to live on the street. It is much too dangerous for the likes of you."

"But Mr. Samuel, me don't belong with fine people."

"We shall see." Samuel closed his eyes.

Graham looked at the child. "Shall we ferret out some food?"

Janey Ann swallowed. "What be fer…ferret?"

"One of my favorite words. It means to find something." Graham touched the young girl's head.

"I be berry hungry, sir. Let us hurry."

Graham took her hand. They walked out of the room toward the kitchen. This time of the morning the kitchen was a beehive of activity. Everyone scurried every which way. Graham and Janey Ann stood just inside the door.

Mrs. Millbe took one look at them. "If you be sitting at the table"—she pointed to an area out of the path of the kitchen's activities—"I be bringing you both your morning meal."

"Nothing fancy, Mrs. Millbe. We want simple food."

The child and Graham moved to a long table made from three boards laid side by side. On both sides of the table were wooden benches running the entire length. He patted a place next to him.

"How about you sit here." The little girl quickly sat down and snuggled close. "What and when did you last eat?"

She shrugged her shoulders. "Not sure. Sometimes bread or apples. Sometimes no food." She sighed.

They sat for a few minutes watching the hurrying and scurrying of the kitchen staff. Janey Ann's eyes grew large as the maids did the bidding of the cook. They laughed and sang, mostly off-key, but no one seemed to mind. The sound of the lads reached them before they were joined by Eel, Jimmy, and Jeb.

Eel called out, "Mrs. Millbe, we ain't ate yet. We be starved. Might you have some chores we can be doing to earn a morning meal?"

The cook stopped on the way to the stove. She turned around and looked at the lads. "The wood box needs to be filled. You three hurry off now. Your eats be waiting for you." Just when the boys were leaving, she hollered out, "Remember, small pieces for the stove."

"Yes," they shouted.

"Mr. Graham need me helping?" Janey Ann said once the boys skipped out the door into the yard.

"Not today, young lady."

"You be sure?"

"Young miss, here be your food." Mrs. Millbe placed a plate with two eggs, bacon and biscuits in front of the child.

"All for me?" Janey Ann sat stiffly.

"Yes, all for you. My name is Mrs. Millbe. I be the cook 'ere. Who be you?"

The child jumped up and extended her hand. "I be Janey Ann."

"Do you have a surname?" Graham reached out to brush the hair from her face.

"What that be?" Janey Ann frowned.

"Last name. You see, my name is Graham Rogers."

"Me be Janey Ann Jakes."

Graham promised himself he would do some checking when he found the time. He hoped he could locate some relatives. She most likely didn't have kinfolk. Maybe Maggie would have some ideas. In reality, the little girl had been on her own, like so many others.

"Let us eat, before our food gets cold. I know I am hungry." Graham reached for his silverware.

He was surprised she knew how to use a knife and fork. She didn't use her fingers. Someone had taught her. He wondered who would have taken the time. She never looked up from her plate, even when the boys came and sat down. Finally, she pushed her clean plate away and leaned back.

"Mrs. Millbe, me be helping clean?" She pointed to the table. "Food be ever so good."

"Yes, you take them dirty dishes and put them in the sink." Mrs. Millbe pointed to a huge tub of soapy water.

After Graham had finished eating, the little girl pulled on his shirt sleeve. "It be time to check on Mr. Samuel. You must put your dishes in the water too."

Graham led the way back to Samuel's room and found him still sleeping. Graham touched Janey Ann's shoulder.

"I will leave you here to watch over our friend. If he needs anything, come out into the hallway. Give a shout for Mr. Barnaby or me."

She nodded her head and again sat on the loveseat. Graham covered her with blankets. Her eyes were closing when he tiptoed out of the room. He almost ran into Barnaby.

"I finally found you. How are our guests? Mrs. Millbe is fascinated with our young guest, as is everyone else. Any idea where or who her family is?"

Graham rubbed his face. "She is yet another mystery added to our list. I believe she made up a surname just to have one. This is a common practice in London. Cannot say the name she gave me will help us find her family, which by the by she says is Jakes."

"The reason I came to get you is we have a KM6 meeting." He pulled out his pocket watch. "We best get moving. We only have one hour to get there. I have a few stops to make along the way. I have informed Hirsch where we are going just in case he needs to contact us."

Barnaby was surprised KM6 (King's Men Six), the secret government agency, was asking for his help. Usually, his partner the Earl was the primary contact. From time to time Barnaby could offer valuable information due to his connections in the East End. Add the associates the Earl could provide and both men had the power to aid KM6 in many delicate situations.

Chapter Seventeen

The next morning, everything seemed back to the usual chaos. Hirsch and Wills converted Samuel's room into a decent bedroom. They removed all the broken furniture and took it to the storage barn on the estate grounds. A beautifully carved wardrobe, a proper bed, a nightstand, and a large dresser now graced the room. A small writing table stood under the only window. Lamps decorated the nightstand, chest of drawers, and the writing table. When all were lit, the room looked inviting, and the glow hid the discolorations on the walls.

Over the next few days, Samuel continued to get stronger. When he managed to hobble into the library to eat, Janey Ann accompanied him. It didn't take him long before he found his way back to his bed.

"I ache all over." He groaned as he moved his leg. "I do not think there is one place that does not hurt."

"You are alive, which is a marvelous thing," Mara said, handing him a glass of water. "My sister says clear, clean water is good for overall health. We boil our drinking water and use a straining cloth to catch any impurities. So please drink every drop."

"Drinking all this just makes me have to go to the—" Samuel shook his head. "I will follow your instructions. However, I do not have to like it."

Barnaby and Graham left and would not reveal

where they were going. There was a constant stream of builders, cabinet makers, floor installers, and painters for Home Sweet Home. All of them needed to review plans and confirm details. Mara knew everyone needed a safe place to live and food to eat. She would not be able to help them all. However, doing whatever she could would be better than wringing her hands about the injustice of it all. She was determined to get the *Ton* to put money in a fund to help finance the home. Mara just had to figure out a way to accomplish such a task. When she had time, she would formulate a plan.

The men finally returned shortly before the evening meal, which would be in the dining room to accommodate the number of people in the house. Samuel managed to shuffle to the table. The children ate in the kitchen with the servants, much to the lads' annoyance.

The topic of conversation, of course, was the events of the last few days. While they had a list of names of people involved, there had to be a leader. The question was who? Would the government take responsibility for part of the situation? Could the authorities be promoting the exit of unwanted homeless people by letting the slave traders transport them to other countries? Would they have just turned a blind eye to what had happened and pretended they were totally unaware of anything just to get rid of the homeless?

Is this why Angell the government man just happened to be involved? Did he aid the slave traders by passing government information to them and protect the evil-doers by withholding information from KM6 about their activities? These questions and many others would never be answered because, as he predicted, someone killed him his first night in Newgate.

It seemed those who could and should help wanted to blame some unknown, unnamed person or persons for this terrible act. Tracking down the list of the people behind these evil doings turned out to be a monumental task. Many of the suspected people had either left town for some unknown destination or were not from London or even England. It didn't take long to discover some names on their list were fictitious. While it was true they caught the men hired to transport the slaves, they really wanted to find the people responsible for funding such an operation. It took a great deal of money to have such a successful venture. At least, for now, the homeless were safe. The hunt would continue until the people responsible were caught.

For a week, Mara and Maggie watched over Samuel and Janey Ann. No one seemed to know where the little girl came from. Even the lads could not find out anything about her family. The child recalled one day she had been on a farm and rode in a hay wagon to the outskirts of London. There a man took her to London Bridge and told her to wait for her aunt whom she had never met. She remembered waiting for a long, long time. Finally, just as evening approached and the lamplighters came, an old woman arrived and took her home where she stayed for a long time. Then one day Janey Ann could not wake the old lady.

Mara was determined to find out where the child was from. It might take a long time to prove or disprove Janey Ann's story, but Mara was determined to do so, no matter how long it took. The next day Janey Ann, Mara, Maggie, the lads, and two bodyguards went to where Janey Ann said she had lived. The boys knocked on the front entrance. When no one answered, Eel went to the back door, ran through the house, and opened the front door. They all moved into a small entryway. Jimmy produced a lantern and they walked through the vacant house.

Mara, however, noticed there did not appear to be any dust anywhere. Someone took good care of the home even if it was empty. The question in her mind remained. There was more to this story. There had to be. Why would someone watch over an empty house and keep it clean? There were no signs anyone stayed in any of the rooms. There were no clothes, no dirty or clean dishes, no food, and no bedding of any kind.

"Are you sure this is the right house?" Mara touched the child's shoulder.

Janey Ann went to the kitchen. She opened a corner cupboard, pushed aside a panel at the back, and brought out a book.

"Her read to me from this. Said to keep it hidden."

"Did she ever say from whom?"

"No, not never. We always had food. Me felt safe until her died." Mara picked up the book and looked into the side panel after the others left the room. She found another book and placed both books into her carry bag. They might provide clues later as to who owned them. She would get to the bottom of this mystery when she had time, which would be much later.

"What happened when she died?" Mara asked.

"The greengrocer came by. When I told him about the lady, he rushed out of the house. Then people come and made me leave. I watched them take me friend away in an old wagon." The child sighed. "I left. Then me found Eel and his mates. When I be alone, and it be dark, I sometimes come back here. I got a place her made for me—a very secret place."

The girl motioned them to follow her. Janey Ann took them outside to a small storage building. She disappeared behind a large bush sitting at the front corner. She stuck her head out. "Come in, there not be much room." She held up a small lantern and held open a trap door. Everyone entered except the guards. Someone had taken great care to make a safe, cozy hiding place for the girl.

"Janey Ann, you can no longer stay here. The slave traders or others like them might come and find you," Mara said. "Is there anything you wish to bring to Woodhaven?"

"We can send the boys for a cart if necessary." Maggie squeezed Janey Ann's shoulder.

The young girl walked around the room. She picked up a few items and set them on the table. "This be all."

Mara found a large tablecloth yellowed with age and placed the items—a cup, a porcelain hairbrush, and a pair of gloves—in the center. Mara pulled the ends of the cloth into the middle and tied them together so the bundle could be carried. They returned home.

The women took Janey Ann to the bedroom they had chosen for her. While they had been gone, the maids, under the supervision of Hirsch, had cleaned and decorated the room for the young girl.

Later in the day Mara and Maggie chatted about the lads. It had become apparent Jimmy and Jeb could no longer live in the old carriage house behind the dress shop. Janey Ann had to have a safe place to live too, or she would be forced at some point to make a living on the streets. Maggie had seen enough of the heartache befalling anyone having to live such a life. She refused to let that happen to Janey Ann. The women conceived an idea, but first, they must have a discussion with Susan.

The women and two bodyguards went to Creations and entered through the back door. While they waited for Susan to finish with a customer, they perused the new yardage delivered late yesterday. One of the seamstresses in the main salon agreed to assist any new clients. She would only come if she required Susan's assistance.

Mara had developed the plans in her head down to the smallest details after her discussion with Maggie. Once Susan arrived, it did not take long for Mara to get to the reason they had come to see her.

"Susan, Maggie and I have an idea—actually a problem—and you can be part of our solution. You do have a right to tell us you want no part of our plan."

Susan sat with her hands in her lap. "I be listening, Miss Mara."

"Well, today we found out where Janey Ann has been living. We also determined it is not safe for Jimmy and Jeb to continue to live in their current location. They could all be prime targets for corrupt, immoral, or dishonest people. Our plan is for you to allow Jimmy and Jeb to live with you. You would receive a monthly fee for their expenses. I would enlarge your living quarters to accommodate them."

Susan sat back in her chair. "The lads are together all the time. They usually have their evening meals here. What about Janey Ann?"

"I am going to talk to Graham about having her live with us. However, she would need to learn a skill or profession to support herself. I want her to attend school. She could become an apprentice in the dress shop or in the herbal center. Over time she could determine what her interests are. I would see she is given every opportunity to be successful in whatever she chooses to do with her life."

"You do not have to give us an answer tonight or tomorrow. If possible, we hope you could make a decision by the end of the week." Mara chewed on her lip. "Please do this because you want to, not because you think you must."

The women agreed over a cup of tea Susan would come to them when she had made a decision regarding Jimmy and Jeb. Mara and Maggie returned to Woodhaven. They found the children entertaining Samuel. Mara shooed them out of the room with a promise of some of Mrs. Millbe's baked sweets. Maggie marched them to the kitchen.

"Thank you. I did not have the heart to tell them to leave. The children were trying so hard to cheer me up."

"I would like to check your wounds and then let you get some much-needed rest."

She retrieved the supplies left on the small sideboard. She re-dressed Samuel's wounds, applying the healing salve to his numerous cuts and bruises. That done, Mara found the children in the kitchen eating scones and drinking tea.

"May I join you? I find I am very, very hungry." Mara sat next to the little girl.

"Yes miss," Jimmy said with a big smile on his face.

The men did not return. The women sat in the library while the children ate their evening meal in the kitchen. Susan joined them to further discuss their plans regarding the children. Susan agreed to have Jimmy and Jeb live with her and Eel if the boys understood they had to mind her, just like Eel. The three women decided no announcement would be made until Maggie talked to Graham about the little girl.

Just when Mara and Maggie had given up hope the men would be back early, they walked through the door. Over their evening meal, Graham agreed to Maggie's proposal of having Janey Ann live with them once Mara's problems were over. Until then, she would live at the Woodhaven Estate.

Hirsch gathered everyone in the library once the couples finished eating. Mara explained Jimmy and Jeb could no longer live in the building behind the shop. The boys started to protest until Mara reminded them about the unsavory types of people recently seen on the docks.

"But miss, where w-we be living?" Jeb stuttered. Tears formed in his eyes.

"Eel, would you like to tell Jimmy and Jeb where their new home will be?"

"Oh yes. You both be living with my mother and me. Both of you will become part of our family."

Both Jimmy and Jeb sat up straight in their chairs, then jumped up and danced around the room with Eel. Once the lads settled down, they sat on the floor near Susan. The little girl had not moved. Janey Ann's eyes had never left her hands lying on her lap.

"Young lady, did you think we forgot about you?" Mara touched the little girl's hand.

"Me did worry some." She still did not look up.

"Miss Maggie is going to discuss your future with you," Mara said.

"When Graham and I return to our home, we would like you to come and live with us."

Janey Ann looked up at Maggie. "Truly, havin' a real home?" She sighed, ran over, and hugged Maggie. "Goin' to school and learnin' many new things?"

"Yes." Maggie beamed at the young girl. "If you find you have an interest in clothing you can become an apprentice to Miss Susan. There are many other opportunities we can discuss."

"Me needs to be thinkin' on that, iffin' I may?"

"Yes, Janey Ann, and it is only one possibility. You see, you may have many interests. You must tell us what they are. Someday you will have to support yourself. Being a dressmaker could be one of those choices. Miss Susan can show you what that means."

"Oh, how can me ever thank all of you? To have a home. A safe place to be. A real home. No longer got to hide from mean people. What name should I be calling you, Miss Maggie and Mr. Graham?"

"What would you like to call us?"

"May I call you mother and father? Should I call you Miss Maggie and Mr. Graham?"

"You pick. I must tell you I do like the sound of mother and Graham would like being called father. You see, we have always had a place in our hearts for a child but never had one. You, my dear little girl, will fill that spot. You will become our daughter."

Janey Ann sat down and cried. Graham rushed over

and picked up her up.

"Do not cry. We did not mean to hurt you in any way."

"Me ain't sad. Me happy and feel safe. Be the first time in a long time." Janey Ann wriggled out of Graham's embrace and ran over to Eel. He grabbed her hand. The children all fled from the room and hurried out to the garden.

The women tried their best to hide their tears.

****

During the next week, the carpenters were busy converting the storage room next to Susan and Eel's lodgings into bedrooms for the boys. Mara felt the lads should have their own room with a large shared room in the center. Each would have privacy, but there would be one place where they could all study together. Once the work was completed, the carriage house behind Creations would be torn down.

Every morning, Susan gathered all the children and went to the dress shop. Janey Ann's excitement at learning to sew was a joy to watch. She proved a natural to do the delicate finish work. Her stitches were small and even. Susan had learned over the years sewing is an art. An apprentice could either do it or not. Within two days Janey Ann's stitching hardly ever needed to be removed or reworked. Creations' business would continue to grow and would require additional workers. Finding someone who could do excellent finish work happened to be one of the most challenging tasks to fulfill.

After the house had quieted down, meaning the lads were in bed and could not overhear their conversation, Mara announced to Graham and Barnaby,

"In two days, you both are invited to accompany Maggie and me to the Duchess of Hempwood's estate."

"We have not found all those involved in directing the slave traders. We are still working with KM6. We cannot—" Barnaby reached out for Mara's hand. She quickly moved it just out of his grasp.

"Yes, you can. It is time to confirm my mother's identity. I need to know who brought me to England and why. I cannot continue to live like this." *There. I have finally said it. No turning back now. I must stand on my own two feet.*

Barnaby said, "We still do not know who tried to kill you and why."

Chapter Eighteen

"They cannot do me harm if they cannot find me," Mara stated. "Why should I wait? The traders have been stopped, at least for the present. It most likely will take time before a new scheme can start again on such a large scale. It could take months or more, even years."

"What about Susan and the children?" Barnaby leaned back in his chair. "Graham, I could use a little help to dissuade Mara from this plan of hers."

"I learned long ago not to argue with Maggie because I never win. I suggest you follow my lead because you cannot win with Mara, either," Graham said. "They are much alike and getting more so every day."

"I do not expect us to be gone long. The Hempwood Estate is not far from here. It takes only one day if we leave very early in the morning. We should return late in the evening. I believe Susan and the children should stay here while we are gone. Hirsch and Wills can watch over them. Susan can take a bodyguard while she is at Creations. Besides, Samuel is up and about now." Mara took a sip of the whiskey Barnaby had just handed to her.

"I must say one thing…" Graham paused to get everyone's attention.

"About time!" Barnaby grumbled.

Graham raised his eyebrows. "I hope we are not

traveling on a fool's errand. How do you know the duchess will see us? I understand she is a recluse and does not see anyone."

"Remember, I have a connection to the duchess from long ago," Maggie said. "She owes me her life. I plan to remind her with a visit."

"I don't understand." Mara's jaw dropped.

"In the East End, when you do something for someone like saving their life, they owe you more than they can ever repay. The duchess will see us, make no mistake."

"What are you saying about saving someone's life?" Graham stood.

"It is not something I care to discuss. I took an oath. I cannot go back on my promise to never speak of…" Maggie sighed.

****

The Woodhaven coach left the house at five in the morning two days later. Everyone grumbled when Mara woke them before dawn. They had all agreed to get an early start. The men still complained. Mara and Maggie chose to ignore them. After she had changed Samuel's dressing. Mara informed him one of the apprentices from the herbal shop would check on him late in the day or, at the latest, in the early evening.

Barnaby and Graham drove the carriage. Wills, the coachman, stayed to watch over Susan and the children. The men flipped a coin for who would drive their transport out of London. Graham lost the toss, so he got the first shift of driving.

"I am looking forward to driving through London in the new carriage. Maneuvering on the roads should be enjoyable," Graham said.

"Ha, you are just uttering those words because you lost the toss. I would bet a farthing you would rather be a passenger." Barnaby laughed out loud.

"Well, I must say I like the bird's eye view I shall have with the reins in my hands."

They walked to the coach and helped the ladies inside. The men were alike in so many ways and in others the opposite, which amused them both.

Barnaby settled back in the squabs and closed his eyes. He was tired of chasing after murderers, cutthroats, and spies. At first, the hunt had been exciting. He did enjoy the satisfaction of bagging the quarry. He really did not know if his age made the difference or the fact that he was sick of seeing the wrong people succeed while hard-working people never seemed to get ahead.

The rocking of the carriage put him to sleep along with Mara and Maggie. All three woke when they heard and felt the coach come to a complete stop. Barnaby raised the curtain. He looked out the window to see where they were. He wanted to make sure they were not being held up. Even in this day and age, there were highwaymen.

A knock on the door announced it was time to change drivers. When Barnaby opened the door, Graham put down the steps.

"I thought everyone would like to walk about and take some nourishment. Your turn to drive." Graham grinned.

Barnaby helped the ladies down from the carriage.

"At the rate we are going we should get there after the midday meal." Barnaby walked around the carriage as he talked, checking to make sure everything remained in working order. "We should only have to make one more stop to rest the horses before we arrive at our destination."

Mara cleared her throat. "Gentlemen, I purchased Cornish pasties and orange flower wine for everyone. I thought we could eat while we traveled. I know we cannot spend a lot of time when we stop." Mara handed both men their food.

"Thank you, Mara. How very thoughtful." Barnaby climbed up to his perch and gathered the reins while everyone climbed into the carriage.

Mara was in awe when they started down the road to the Hempwood Estate. The manor house looked enormous and impressive when it came into view. It made Woodhaven look like a summer cottage. The sun glistened on the façade. The four-story estate was magnificent. Driving down the long entrance, she glimpsed a large building standing behind the manor house. Horses were tied to a hitching rail in front of a barn. A riding facility stood off in the distance. A large pond sat off to the north side of the house. A group of swans glided across the smooth surface. The closer they got to the house, the more nervous Mara became. She blinked her eyes, trying her best to hide her emotions. There were so many questions and so many what-ifs running through her mind.

Mara and Maggie approached the door and used the shiny brass knocker to announce their arrival. When a man dressed in livery answered the door. Maggie stepped forward and presented her card. Barnaby and Graham stood with the carriage.

"We are here to see the Duchess of Hempwood. It is urgent we speak with her. I am sure she will meet with us."

The man moved to get a good look at Barnaby and Graham standing with the horses. He then looked directly at Mara. "You must wait here. I will inquire if she is receiving guests at this time of day."

Before either of the women could reply, the servant bowed his head and shut the door. They both heard the click of the door being locked and his heavy footsteps scurrying away. He returned within minutes.

"The Duchess of Hempwood agrees to receive Miss Margaret Marker-Rogers and no one else."

Maggie grabbed Mara's hand and whispered, "Do not be nervous. Everything will be all right."

Mara walked down the two steps to Barnaby and Graham. The men talked in whispers. Graham motioned for Mara to follow them. They went to the front door and found it locked. Barnaby put his fingers to his lips and looked at Mara. He took his lock picks out of his pocket.

"Wait. What if the duchess gets angry and refuses to even talk to us or me? This plan of yours could ruin my chances of ever finding out anything. Maybe we should wait."

"Mara, this is the only possibility. If Maggie comes out there will be no meeting with the duchess." Barnaby opened the door.

Mara sighed profoundly and followed him. On tiptoes, all three walked into the foyer. They listened carefully. Barnaby pointed to a closed, carved double door at the end of a long hallway. Very quietly, they moved until they were standing at the center of the doors.

Barnaby put his closed fist up in the air, raised one

finger, then a second finger, and then raised a third finger. He reached down and opened the door. Barnaby gently maneuvered Mara into the room, hoping the sight of her would stop the duchess from having them all thrown out. Barnaby and Graham walked in behind Mara and closed the door.

She straightened her back, trying to look as tall as possible. Mara ran her hands down her skirt trying to smooth out the wrinkles. The dust from their travels seemed to mentally and physically weigh her down. This might be her only opportunity. She found it hard to believe she had come this far. The meek and mild woman who had always let her older sister fight her battles had evaporated. Now she had to think on her feet. No longer could she mull over every detail for days or weeks. Finally, she was learning to think quickly.

"Your Grace, I believe I have grown up since you last saw me. I have something I wish to show you. My foster mother sent this recently." Mara handed over the blue bag.

She moved back a few feet. Barnaby and Graham stepped forward to stand next to her.

"I should be angry at you and these men." The duchess pointed to the trio standing in front of her. "You all have entered my home uninvited. But if you had sent a message…"

Suddenly the doors were thrown open. Men with pistols stood in the doorway. Barnaby and Graham turned to face them. Barnaby pushed Mara behind him. Graham moved to stand in front of Maggie.

The duchess motioned to the men in the doorway. "These people mean no harm. Make sure no one else comes into the house."

The taller of the four men took two steps forward. The duchess said "*J'en suis sure.*"

The men bowed their heads. They backed out of the room and shut the door.

Barnaby took Mara's hand and whispered in her ear, "She told them I am safe." He raised his voice. "I am sure they are guarding the door. Am I right Madam?"

"Yes, you are correct. I should have all of you thrown out." She waved her lorgnette at them. "Margaret, now tell me why you have come. What is the world coming to when visitors do not send cards to inform people they are going to make an afternoon call? Did you think I would refuse you?"

"I did!" Maggie walked over to stand next to Mara.

"You are right. I would have. But you are here now, so do tell me why you have come." The duchess leaned over and handed the bag back to Mara. "Do sit down. I hate looking up at people. You make me tired." She reached out toward the bell pull. "I shall order some refreshments. You all look thirsty. I think something to drink is in order."

"Thank you," said Barnaby.

"While we are waiting, I do have an idea why you have appeared. But I would rather you tell me. It saves misunderstandings."

Mara cleared her throat. She proceeded to tell the duchess all that happened before the end of the last year. She started with Mrs. Pearly's party, the murder attempts on herself and Susan, then added the fact she had asked her foster mother if she could identify the person or persons who had delivered her on that stormy night.

The refreshments arrived. After everyone had been served, Mara felt her tears forming in her eyes as her chin quivered. She would not give up since she had come so far. Mara was the only one who could and should ask the questions which needed to be asked.

"Why should I offer information to you? You are nothing to me. I really do not owe you anything."

Mara took a deep breath and pushed back her shoulders. She placed her teacup on the table and rose from her chair.

I can do this. The worst that can happen is my dear friends and I will be thrown out.

"Madam, you are right. You owe me nothing. I am one woman seeking to find out who my birth parents are. I suppose you would not understand." Mara spread her arms out to cover the entire room. "You have a family history. When you walk up the stairs"—she pointed to the door—"there is a gallery of portraits of your family going back hundreds of years. All I have is a stunning and expensive necklace. No one knows the identity of my father. However, you have information you wish to keep to yourself. There is nothing I can do about it. Thank you for your time and the refreshments. It is time we leave. Goodbye."

Mara turned, her head held high, and walked to the door. Barnaby, Graham, and Maggie were right behind her. She placed her shaking hand on the doorknob.

"Stop," shouted the duchess. "I never thought this day would come. Oh, how you are like your mother. At first, I believed you were somebody who had heard one of the rumors. You are not the first to come and want to trade gossip for facts. You are the first to arrive with the diamond necklace given to Catherine Highbridge for your care. I knew when I saw the bag I picked the right person to raise you.

"I have watched you from afar for years. Gather some chairs around my desk. I am going to tell you this story only once. I do not plan to repeat the tale for you or anyone else again." She set her lorgnette down and cleared her throat.

Chapter Nineteen

Mara had no idea where the chair came from until the pressure against the back of her legs forced her to sit down. The duchess sat directly across from her. Out of the corner of her eye, she saw Barnaby sitting next to her, Maggie on the other side of her, and then Graham.

"The ordinary French people hated and distrusted the French monarchy long before the French Revolution. Once the mob and rioters took over, there was no going back for anyone. By the time I received word of the chaos, I could not go to support your mother who was a member of the French court. I had no way to contact her and no idea what I could have done. In fact, I had no idea where she was being kept. Six months before the beheading started, I received a frantic message from someone who will remain nameless. The missive was short and heartbreaking. No one would be spared. Months later I received a second message. One of the women in the cells informed me your mother would soon be having a baby. She believed the baby would be killed unless I could devise a way to rescue the infant and bring the child to England to be raised.

"Your mother and I lived in Paris. Our mothers were prostitutes, and in truth, we were raised in the same fashion. When my mother died, I had the opportunity to leave Paris. A cousin from England came to get me. My life was not much better until I met my duke. He was old enough to be my father and treated me like his daughter. But that story is for another time and place.

"Three bodyguards, myself, and a very trusted English friend who looked at this as the adventure of a lifetime traveled to Paris about three weeks before your birth. You were your mother's first child. We were not sure when you would come into this turbulent world. The women of the court had fallen from grace along with their queen. They lived in terrible circumstances. They had little food. Conditions of life were degrading, and unhealthy. We needed to be ready when you made your grand entrance. My friend's family owned land in and around Paris including buildings, houses, and storage facilities. I believe this saved our lives more than once. We waited and waited. The week before your birth, the rioting and mobs of bloodthirsty Parisians kept us on the move. We never stayed in one place more than one night. I still have nightmares.

"Early in the morning hours, a crippled male servant and a young girl brought you to us. You were not more than a few hours old. We made our escape in a falling apart old cart. How it held together none of us ever understood; it creaked, and the wheels wobbled, and the hay stank like cow manure. I never figured out how we managed to make it past the roaming bands of cutthroats and thieves. For three days we did not get much sleep. We finally made it to the docks, and I have never been so glad to see a ship in all my life. We had to run before a mob of looters caught up to us. The young girl who brought you to us left into the dark night along with the male servant. With them was a wet nurse who had been with you since your birth. We did not ask any questions as there was no time. We escaped because the ship's many sailors were armed. They were willing and able to kill anyone who tried to follow us aboard the vessel. I stood on the deck, peering into the dark night, watching for the English coast. You were such a good baby. You did not cry and hardly made a sound the entire trip. Upon our arrival in London your nurse left in the dead of night. We tried to find her and could not.

"I doubt the public ever knew a lady-in-waiting had birthed a child a few days before her execution. Your mother's name was Theresa Mercier."

The duchess drank the last of her tea and leaned back in her chair. "There is one way you can prove you are the child I saved. The men must turn around and face the door."

Barnaby cleared his throat. "Why such a request, Duchess?"

"The child I brought to England had a birthmark on her left hip. When you turn around, Mara may show it to me."

Barnaby stood and walked over to Graham. "Come, it is time for us to look at this great hand-carved door." The men strolled over and stood in front of the entrance to the room.

Mara quickly walked over and pulled up her skirt. The duchess saw the star on her left hip.

"You, my dear, are the child. I do so wish your mother could see you." She reached out and hugged Mara. "Gentlemen, you may turn around. Mara is the child I brought from France."

"Do you have any idea who my father could be?"

Mara crossed her fingers.

"No, sad to say. I did not have an opportunity to speak to Theresa or to the young maid who brought you to me. I had not been to France for many years, nor do I think you should go. Your mother was involved in many events and incidents, many of which were not legal. You look enough like her for someone to notice. In England, you can claim you might have relatives in France but do not know who they are."

"I would like to know if you ever heard of 'The Affair of the Diamond Necklace.'" Barnaby narrowed his eyes. "We believe, Graham and I, the diamond pendant that was given to Catherine Highbridge might be part of the necklace. The teardrop diamond matches a drawing we acquired."

"This is what I know and believe. Your mother and father most likely had a part in the theft of the necklace—by now worth millions of pounds. I do not remember all the details.

"It involved many people: a cardinal who wanted to become a member of the court, a prostitute, and a con man. There were many variations of the necklace's story. Some I am sure was true and others…Well, just deceptions to lead people away from the truth. It became the talk of France and one of the reasons the French people came to hate the queen. Be very careful because the necklace is still missing. It is still out there somewhere. And yes, I believe the diamond your foster mother received could be from the necklace."

"I wish we had more time. I am not sure what to do with all the information you have shared with us. Thank you, Duchess." Mara brushed the tears from her eyes.

"Would you all leave and wait for Mara by your

coach? I have one last piece of information I wish to convey to her."

Maggie hurried over to the duchess and gave her a hug. "Thank you, Brigit. I am sorry we had to infringe on your privacy. However, it was necessary. Please accept our condolences on the death of your husband, the duke."

"Dearest Margaret, your mother remained a dear friend to me. You are as well. I am glad you came. I have also watched you from afar. I must say I wondered when you married Graham if it had been a wise choice. I see it was the best thing for both of you. Be happy, my dear. Life changes so quickly. I am most pleased you are not in the business like your mother. Take care, and if you ever need me again, just come. I promise to always receive you with open arms."

Once Mara's friends walked out, the duchess said, "I would be remiss if I did not inquire about your future plans. I could see the man, I believe you called him Barnaby, looking at you with longing."

"Yes, Barnaby and I are close friends at this point. Our attraction is becoming love. I hope it is. He is everything I want in a man: honest, kind, brave, thoughtful, and my protector. My only problem is he believes I need someone with a title. I must tell you I have a very successful dress shop in London. Of course, the *Ton* is not privy to the fact I own it—which I have found makes it all the more fun. It is my little secret. However, shortly, I do want to settle down and have a family. I am hopeful my life can continue with Barnaby at my side. Time will tell what my future will be. However, for the first time I am reaching out and becoming a voice to be heard. Thank you, dear lady, for taking the time to tell my story. What you have said to me is our secret." She handed the duchess her card, and on the back, Mara had hand-written the name of her shop. "If you ever need my assistance, please contact me."

The duchess tugged on the bell pull. When the butler came in, she said, "Tell the people out by the carriage to wait for an armed escort. We have had highwaymen in the area."

When they returned home, they discovered everyone was in bed. Hirsch met them at the door with his pistol in hand. The two couples went to the library for a drink. They had further plans to make.

Barnaby, Graham, and Samuel left at sunrise. They had important business to discuss with the KM6 men.

Chapter Twenty

The women were enjoying their second cup of tea in the cozy library when the men returned. The boys and Janey Ann were eating at the kitchen table. Both men stood tall, their movements relaxed as they walked through the door. Then they slapped each other on the back and grinned from ear to ear.

"You both seem overly happy. I hope good news." Mara stretched over to the bell pull to order breakfast.

Barnaby hurried across the room toward the fireplace to warm his hands. The weather had turned bitterly cold. "By late this afternoon, all the people living in England who are involved in the human trafficking will be arrested. I believe most will hang. I cannot say I am sorry. Transportation to Australia or some other outpost would not stop them from their activities. They would just continue their dastardly deeds by using different locations and names. Our government officials hope their fate will send a message to the world. This type of behavior is considered the worst criminal activity against humankind. England will not tolerate it here nor in any of the countries it governs."

Mrs. Millbe promised to make a special meal for an early evening celebration so everyone could take part, even the children. Mara was determined to accompany Susan to the shop. Maggie needed to go home and make sure everything there continued to run smoothly. Barnaby and Graham decided to pursue the information they had received about the necklace. In truth, they wanted to verify some of the details. Eel, Jimmy, Jeb, and Janey Ann left for school. They agreed to come by the dress shop when they were done for the day.

Two bodyguards went with Mara and Susan. One Bow Street Runner went with Maggie as she had errands to do. The women promised to return to the manor no later than six in the evening.

The Woodhaven carriage turned into the mews behind the shop. One of the guards jumped down and proceeded to inspect Creations. When he returned, the women walked into the building. Susan went upstairs to feed the cat who had recently become part of the family. He turned out to be the best mouser she had ever had. The cat ran around her feet until she picked him up.

Mara went to her locked office and opened the door. A man sat in her chair. For reasons she could not explain to herself later, she was not afraid. She cleared her throat to get the man's attention as his eyes were closed.

"May I help you?" She chewed on her lower lip.

The man jumped as his eyes opened. "I-I am not here to harm you. I needed to speak to you in private. There didn't appear to be any other way. So here I am. Do not shout out to anyone. It would only ruin my surprise."

"I will not. But you must know there are people here to protect me."

"Yes, Mara. I know your schedule almost as well

as you do yourself. I have tried for a long time to meet you but there is always someone with you. I am a wanted man. Many people are looking for me. Time is running out. I must get to the point."

"Would you like a cup of tea? I find I am still thirsty this morning." Her throat was so dry, she could hardly swallow or think.

"I would appreciate that, daughter of my heart."

Mara turned to open the door and swiveled back. "What did you just say?"

"You are the daughter of my heart. I must tell you. I have looked for you for years."

Mara motioned him to stand behind the door. "Susan," she called. "Would you come here?"

When Susan stood at the edge of the door, Mara asked sweetly, "Would you please bring me a pot of tea and two cups? I just realized I am expecting a visitor."

"Yes, miss. I have already put the kettle on." Susan left and returned shortly with tea and a small plate of biscuits.

Mara poured the refreshments with a shaky hand. The man moved to sit in the chair.

"My name is Peter Dumont. I was formerly a servant in the French court. I fell in love with your mother, and for some reason, she with me. We could not marry due to our stations in life, or so I thought. Years later, I realized she had been no better born than me. I do not mean to sound bitter. If only I had known more, we all might have had a life together. Now I have an illness that cannot be cured." Peter shook his head when Mara tried to speak. "I must finish before you ask me any questions. I came to give you the only possession I own that has any worth.

"Your mother and I fooled a large number of people. I pretended to be an old, crippled manservant to stay near the beautiful young lady-in-waiting. Looking back, I am not proud of what we did. In reality, the French Revolution removed the real ownership of my—our—gift to you."

Peter handed Mara a tall square box that fit in the palm of her hand.

"What is it and why are you giving this to me?"

"It is all I have to give you. It actually fell into our laps, your mother's and mine. At the time, we had no idea what secret the hand-held, small, rounded, covered old chest held until we opened it.

"One minute we were figuring out what to do. Theresa was going to have my child, and I was merely a servant with no real future because France was coming apart at the seams. People were killing neighbors and friends. Everything changed almost overnight for us. Then we found an elaborate container in her room with no note or instructions.

"There had been rumors about the necklace floating around France for a few years. It is still much talked about. No one knew who had it or where it had gone, just that it was missing. The people thought to be responsible were all acquitted except for one. She escaped prison and is believed to be hiding in England."

"Peter—you are my father? I thought I would never have the opportunity to meet you. I can help you. I would like to spend time to get to know you and learn about my mother."

"I am afraid, my dearest daughter of my heart, it is not possible. I must leave. I am dying. I do not wish you to see what will become of me. Remember me like this. I only ask one thing. Do not give the contents of the box to anyone from France claiming it belongs to them. It does not. It is yours to start your life with Barnaby. The money for these precious stones will be the beginning of your family's fortune. With this, you can help many unfortunate people. You can give them hope when they have none. Remember me with the fondest of memories. My dear, oh, how I wish I had time to spend with you."

I find for the first time in my life no words to express my inner thoughts. My heart and mind are in a turmoil that until now has never existed. I feel like a ship sinking in a stormy sea. I don't know if I should hug him or hate him. I wanted to know him all my life. Now I am only going to have a few minutes which will have to last a lifetime.

Tears rolled down Mara's face. "This is not how I expected to meet you. In fact, I was not sure I would ever have the privilege. Yet now I find I am losing you before I get to know and love you. Are you so confident we cannot discover a way to resolve the issues preventing us from being a family even for a day?" She wiped the tears from her eyes.

Peter stood. "What you ask is impossible. You are what your mother and I hoped you would be—a wonderful, caring woman. You have a bright future ahead of you. Enjoy your life. It passes very quickly. I must go."

"How can you leave? There are guards. They will stop you."

He reached out and hugged Mara tightly "No, I am all right." He moved the chair over against the outer door, took the corner of the rug that had been under the chair, and laid it back over itself. He then took a knife from the scabbard on his side and stuck it into the floor and pulled upward. A trap door opened up. He reached down with his hands and lowered himself into the hole. His head stuck out above the floor.

Mara dropped down to her hands and knees. "How did you—? When did you—?" She reached out and kissed both of his cheeks. "Goodbye, Father. I have a special place in my heart for you, now and forever. I love you."

She stood there, tears running down her cheeks once he was gone from view. She closed the trap door, put the rug and chair back in place. She opened the box and could not believe her eyes. It contained diamonds and sapphires. She knew they were the stones of the necklace.

She went to the door and called to one of the bodyguards. She told him to find Barnaby, Graham, and Maggie. "It is important they come immediately. It is most urgent they come to Creations post-haste."

She sat, cried, and cried some more. She drank all the tea. Once her father started talking, she had forgotten about their refreshments. Mara hid the box inside the trash bin under her desk, then hurried to the necessary, and locked the door behind her. She reached up for the loaded pistol she kept there on a little recessed shelf behind a few bottles of clothing dye.

Suddenly she heard shouting from the front of the shop. She walked slowly and deliberately to the main salon and stopped. Two men stood just inside the closed front door.

Susan stood in front of the visitors trying to block their advance into Creations. The bodyguard stood off to one side, observing, and then started to move forward.

Chapter Twenty-One

Barnaby pushed open the front door. The visitors moved aside. The bodyguard shifted closer to Susan. He stayed out of sight. Mara scooted further back into the fitting room, the pistol held at her side.

"We have more men in the shop than women today," Susan said, with a hint of nervous laughter in her voice.

One of the visitors bowed his head. "I am looking for a person from France. I believe he acquired stolen property belonging to the French government. I wish to search the premises."

"Who are you?" Barnaby clenched his fists at his sides.

"I would like to talk to the owner of this establishment," the man said with flared nostrils.

"The owner currently is not here. I be the manager," Susan announced.

At that moment, Graham and Maggie walked into the shop.

"Well, well, well. Look who is here, my dear wife."

"Jacko, when did you get out of the Bastille?" Maggie said.

"It is time you gentlemen leave." Barnaby crossed his arms over his chest.

"This is not finished. Next time I will bring more

men. Be assured we are coming back. Sooner rather than later. We have unfinished business with the owner of this shop. Be glad she is not here." Jacko stormed out, followed by the second man.

"Susan, lock the door. Where is Mara?" Barnaby walked to the window to make sure the intruders had left.

"I am here." She came out from behind the screen.

"We must go to Woodhaven. I have the reason those men came here," Mara announced. "We must leave now. Let me get my coat."

"Perhaps Mara might offer some idea why she needed us here." Graham took hold of Maggie's hand.

"Come with me. I must retrieve something from my office. It concerns something I encountered today, or I guess I should say, someone."

When Mara showed them the trap door, they all stood with their mouths wide open.

"How the hell did someone do this right under our noses? Did the guards we hired sleep through their shifts? Could they have been bribed?" Barnaby slammed his fist on the desk.

"Mara, who could have done this?" Maggie asked.

"This gun is too heavy to carry around." Mara set it on the desk. "My father made or had the trap door made. Let me retrieve what I came for and we can leave. You will never believe what happened."

"Who did you say? I must have misunderstood." Barnaby said.

"I met my father today. Right here in my office." Mara reached into the trash bin and retrieved the box. She put it in her carry bag and picked up the gun. "Unless either of you is carrying a weapon, you might need this on the way home." She handed it to Barnaby.

The bodyguard stopped her from walking out. "Miss, let me make sure it is safe."

She sighed and stood back while Barnaby and Graham went out first.

Barnaby returned in seconds. "Come, ladies, it is time to go to Woodhaven."

Graham took the pistol from Barnaby. He planned to be the lookout and sit with Wills the carriage driver. Mara started to say something on the drive, but Maggie shook her head.

"Too many ears listening."

The women waited in the carriage with one of the bodyguards. The second guard was to stay at Creations until Barnaby and Graham returned with others to fix the trap door. Barnaby escorted the ladies into the manor house and walked back out with Hirsch, who still carried his pistol.

The butler announced he would go to the school to escort the children home. A Bow Street Runner would accompany him.

The ladies hurried to the library. Mara requested Ivy to bring coffee and sweets.

Wills drove the coach to the stables. Barnaby and Graham walked into the library. Both men were more than curious and wanted details.

By the time the men sauntered into the library, Mara and Maggie had glasses of whiskey on the desk for them. Each man claimed a drink, then sat down and waited for what seemed like forever. Finally, Barnaby cleared his throat.

"Mara, are you going to tell us what happened? We have to get back to fix the trap door and secure your shop."

"At the first opportunity, Jacko will return and plow through Creations, destroying everything in his path," Graham said.

Mara sighed. "You are never going to believe what happened."

They all looked at her, then started to talk at the same time. She held up her hands, palms outward, to stop them. "One at a time, please."

The refreshments arrived, but no one made a move. Maggie asked Ivy to close the curtains.

Mara explained what had happened and what her father had told her. Then she opened her carry bag and took out the box. She asked Barnaby to bring her the plate the sweets were on. Of course, he brought the desserts and the dish. She took the plate and dumped everything onto a napkin. After she put a biscuit in her mouth, Mara upended the box, pouring the contents onto the plate. No one said a word. Everyone just sat and looked at the jewels.

"He said they belong to me. It is my legacy from my parents. This is to be the start of my and Barnaby's family fortune."

"He used my name? How could he know about me?"

"I believe the duchess contacted him, or he contacted her. Remember, my mother and she were childhood friends. I understand what he wants me to do with these jewels. How do you get them to be money? I can't go around giving people a diamond for goods."

Barnaby, Graham, and Maggie all started to chuckle.

"I don't understand…" Mara looked at the trio.

"How can you find this amusing?"

Barnaby took Mara's hand. "Graham is the man who can take diamonds and turn them into money. It is what he does for a living."

"I thought you told me he had been a thief. In fact, you were too at one time in your life. I was under the impression it was all in the past."

"I need to explain," Graham said. "I no longer steal from people, governments or anyone else. I still keep my hands in the pot, so to speak, by converting precious or semi-precious stones into cash. You would be amazed at the number of people who have taken family heirlooms worth millions of pounds, then have the real stones removed, and replaced with excellent fake ones. They do it because they need the money. For many, it is because of gambling debts or foolish spending. This way no one will know they are selling the families' jewels, which in many cases have been in the family for hundreds of years. They have the fake stones mounted into the old settings, and most people can't tell the difference. Some of my customers want to recover what has been stolen or sold by people when they inherit. They will pay enormous amounts of money to get their property returned."

Graham pulled his jeweler's loupe out of his pocket, picked up a sapphire, and proceeded to examine it. "This is one of the best stones I have ever seen. Let me look at one of the diamonds." He placed one in the palm of his hand and turned it over and over, scrutinizing it. "Again, one of the best diamonds I have ever seen."

"My father also told me to use the money to help people. He knows what I have been doing with the school and Home Sweet Home. He did not mention them by name but implied I should continue what I am doing."

"Why did he have to leave?" Maggie touched her arm.

Tears gathered in Mara's eyes. "He said the doctors did not give him much time."

"I cannot do anything with the stones for a while. They are what is called in the trade 'too hot,' which means someone, and I would bet more than one person, is on the lookout for them. Do you have a safe place to hide them? Make no mistake, the villains will come looking for them. Once the stones have left your possession, there will be no trace of the thieves, and you will never be able to find the diamonds or the people who have stolen them. It might be best to split them up and hide them in different places."

"Graham, thank you. I do appreciate your thoughts and advice." Mara placed her hand on her chest.

"I suggest we help Mara divide up the stones. Graham, you know what stones to put together. We could make up packets tonight, right now. We do not want to do this if we are rushed," Barnaby said. "Sounds like a good plan. Mara, do you have any material here at Woodhaven or any bags that are sturdy?"

"Yes, in the herbal room. I am sure there are some there. Let me go—"

Hirsch threw open the library doors with such force they crashed against the bookcases. "People are moving around upstairs. I was leaving to get the children when I heard noises overhead."

"Go get the Runners. Take the children to

Creations," Barnaby said.

Mara grabbed three napkins and poured diamonds in each one. "You two keep talking. Maggie and I will be right back. Check to make sure I have not left any stones behind." Maggie grabbed a lamp.

"Where are you going with these? You cannot just—" Barnaby watched Mara open a secret door next to the fireplace and motion for Maggie to follow her. "Well, do you see what I see? She is amazing."

"That is an understatement." Graham slapped Barnaby's back. "Mara and Maggie are so much alike it scares me."

"Mara, are there more than two entrances?" Barnaby asked.

"Yes. There are two other rooms like this. I can show you the next time we are alone."

The ladies left, and the door closed behind them.

They walked a short distance into a very narrow hallway. The air was stale and almost non-existent. Maggie walked in right behind Mara with her hand on her shoulder due to the darkness. Once Mara lit a lamp, Maggie removed her hand. Finally, Mara inched along the hall until she found a small bookcase sitting about halfway down the narrow path. Mara moved the empty cabinet a few inches to the right. She felt along the wall until she found a small panel and pushed it open. Mara placed the napkins in the opening and pulled the panel back in place. With the bookcase back in its original location, she maneuvered two large clay pots to each side. Using her hands, Mara moved the dust on the floor around until it obliterated the signs that anything had been moved. With a broom from the end of the hallway, Maggie swept the entire area, removing their footprints.

Mara made sure the carafes appeared to have been standing in one place for years by throwing dust on them and eliminating any handprints. They silently returned to the men.

"You have some explaining to do." Barnaby took Mara's hand and gave it a squeeze.

"Whatever do you mean?" Mara giggled.

They moved their chairs around the small table and started to play cards when the door burst open. Everyone turned to look at three men standing in the doorway. Their weapons pointed at the two couples.

"Jacko, now would be a good time to tell us what you have been doing since we saw you last. Would you like a drink? Would you care to join our game?" Barnaby stood.

"I do not like your humor, Mr. Roget. We met in Paris many years ago, during or after the revolution. Only you used a different name. You were called Gage, and someone with you used the name André."

"It is possible… Graham can speak for himself."

"Yes, I was there too. Rather good of you to remember."

"You ruined many of my best plans." Jacko thrust out his chest and stood with his legs in a wide stance. "You cannot outwit me today. Enough of this foolishness. We have come for the jewels."

"Jewels? I have this bracelet." Mara held up her arm. "I am afraid it is not worth much."

"We can kill you if you do not give us what we want."

"Who are you?" Mara took a sip of tea.

"The necklace belongs to me. Someone stole it. I have tracked it for years. Peter was my partner until the woman he loved turned him into a sniveling coward."

"I know nothing about a necklace, nor have I seen one. Why would someone named Peter give such an item to me?"

"You are his daughter, his illegitimate daughter, born of a prostitute."

"I have heard enough nonsense," Mara said, leveling a pistol from behind her back at the men.

Barnaby, Graham, and Maggie stood with weapons readied as well.

"If you don't drop your gun, I will shoot you dead, Jacko. I am an expert shot. Make no mistake. I am not afraid of you or the men with you."

The Runners crept into the room. They stood behind the trio and hit them with their clubs, knocking them out.

"You came in at the right moment, gentlemen." Mara threw her pistol on the closest chair.

"Mara, you must be careful with loaded guns," Maggie said, setting the one in her hand carefully next to Mara's.

"Not to worry. The pistols are not loaded."

Barnaby and Graham looked at each other and shook their heads.

"There was not enough time." Mara sank into the nearest chair.

"Let us help the Runners take these men to Newgate."

Barnaby walked over to the unconscious men. Graham joined him. Hirsch showed up with some rope and tied the men's hands behind their backs, just as they were waking up.

Barnaby threw some water in their faces to speed

their recovery. "It is much easier to move men when they can walk."

"Mara, do not leave the house until we return."

"Why can I not go to the shop?"

"Mara, promise me."

She sighed. "I can wait right here with Maggie. I do not want to, but I shall."

"No one is to leave the house until we come back. No one." Barnaby took the loaded pistol Graham gave him.

The prisoners were placed on the floor of the carriage with the Runners sitting on the seats. Barnaby sat next to Wills, who handled the horses with ease. Graham sat perched on the back of the carriage.

Mara felt a huge weight had been lifted from her shoulders. She no longer had to worry about people trying to do her and her friends harm. However, there were still questions to be asked and answers to be found.

Chapter Twenty-Two

Mara paced the library, waiting for the men to return. She was worried Jacko somehow would once again elude the authorities. When the men returned, they assured the ladies Jacko and his cohorts were secured in their cells, and not just for trying to harm Mara. They had been spies for Napoleon during the war. The British government had a long-standing reward out for the capture of Jacko, as did France and a few others. His days of running and hiding were over, and he would likely be hanged.

Mrs. Millbe and Hirsch decked out the dining room for a celebration. Everyone could breathe more easily now. The man could no longer harm Mara, although only the two couples knew about Jacko and what he stood for.

The value of the necklace and its parts was too high, either in part or whole, for more people not to be pursuing it. Barnaby and Graham suggested it would be in all their best interests if they investigated further.

Late in the evening, after everyone but the two couples had gone to bed, Barnaby informed Mara her father had died of what seemed to be natural causes. He had lived down near the docks. Mara wanted to cry with regret that she had never had the opportunity to build a relationship with him.

Mara knew she would always remember the day

she met her father with fondness. Yet she wondered if he really was her father. She remembered with clarity, when she thought back, how he had said he loved her mother and how Theresa loved him. Yet he called her the daughter of his heart, not just his daughter.

Mara, of course, was grateful for his gift of the diamonds. It would remain to be seen if they would ever bring her and Barnaby any wealth. After all, they were ill-gotten goods. Yet she promised herself she would remain stoic. She would, of course, arrange for his funeral. It would be a quiet affair.

Barnaby and Mara stayed up after Maggie and Graham had gone to bed. They had plans to make.

"Barnaby, do you think Peter was really my father or did I just assume he was because of his gift? I love him with my whole being even if I only had a few minutes to spend with him. He seemed so sincere."

"Mara, I wish I had answers for you, but I do not. I think he loved you, otherwise why would he have given you such a gift?"

Peter was buried the next afternoon in a small cemetery outside London in a very private ceremony with only Mara, Barnaby, Maggie, and Graham in attendance. The cloudy day was fitting for this somber task. Mara's chin trembled, and she stared down at her hands while they stood in the cemetery. After the funeral, they went to the little deteriorating boarding house where Barnaby found Peter had been staying. Graham and Maggie remained in the dim-lit hallway while Mara and Barnaby went into his room. He had a small satchel hidden under some clothes. They packed up his few belongings. Barnaby went to investigate the loud voices they heard coming from the hallway. He instructed Mara to stay in the room until he came for her.

She sighed, looking around the dim, dank area. Curiosity got the best of her. She walked over to the straw mattress and picked up a corner. She pulled it back as far as it would go. A cloth-covered book sat on one of the wooden slats used to keep the mattress off the floor. She put it in her carry bag. She had just finished looking at all the other corners and determined there was nothing else but bugs and dirt when Barnaby opened the door.

"Come, Mara. It was just some drunken men wanting Maggie to go with them. We finally sent them on their way."

The wind came up as they started for home. Mara could feel moisture on her cheeks and knew the rain wasn't far behind. In no time, raindrops began falling, and the air started to smell clean and fresh.

Once Mara got home, she took care of Samuel and then went with a bodyguard to Creations. She sat in her office and read the book she had found. Once finished, Mara put Peter's tattered journal back in her bag for safe keeping. She could not share it with Barnaby or the others today. It was a somber read and broke her heart for her mother and Peter. She could not think of her birth family anymore. They were gone. Now it was time to look forward, not back. With that clear thought in her mind, she hoped her light-hearted attitude would return. Her mood, however, continued to match the dreary weather.

She sat for the longest time, thinking of her future. Not long ago she had planned it all. In time she learned people changed. Everything was not always under her control. She was getting good at taking charge, or at least she thought she was.

So, with that in mind, she sent a letter to her foster father requesting his help in procuring a special marriage license for her and Barnaby. After much discussion, they did not, or rather she did not, want all the hubbub involved in a society wedding.

The couple planned to be gone for a fortnight. Mara found it hard not to tell Susan when they discussed Creations business. When Susan asked if she were going away, Mara assured her store manager she would be busy with Home Sweet Home and would not be coming into the shop for a few days.

Wills, the Woodhaven coach driver, knew of their plans. He was to drive them to the local carriage shop, which rented all manner of vehicles.

Barnaby and Mara met on the stairway the night before their planned departure.

"Mara, are you sure everyone is sleeping?"

"Yes, I waited and waited for the maids to go to their rooms. Maggie and Susan are sleeping. I just checked. We must be quiet."

The words were no sooner out of her mouth when Barnaby walked right into the table in the hallway. The turned-down lantern wobbled until Mara snatched it off the table.

"Did you not hear? We must be quiet," Mara whispered to Barnaby. She put her fingers to her lips. "Silence."

Barnaby carried both travel bags and followed close behind Mara. Footsteps sounded on the stairs. Mara moved into a vacant bedroom and pulled Barnaby inside with her just in time. They backed farther into the darkened room.

"Who left this door open? I be talking to Ivy in the morning." They heard the door being shut. With all the problems, Mara had been having Hirsch check the house at least three times per night.

In a few minutes, they heard Hirsch start down the stairs. When he got to the bottom, they heard him check the front door, and then stroll toward his room at the side of the house.

On tip-toes, the couple started toward the kitchen, far from Hirsch's room. They listened for sounds of anyone up and about.

Mara was grateful for the ray of moonlight coming through the windows. She could hear Mrs. Millbe snore as she passed her room. Mara smelled the loaves of bread rising on the back of the stove. She opened the kitchen service entrance inch by inch in case it squeaked. Once the doors were open, the house cat darted into the room. Mara covered her mouth with one hand. She put the other over her heart and blew out a breath.

"It is only the cat," Barnaby whispered moments before he snickered.

"I see no humor in my being scared." She poked him in the stomach.

They left the house, closing the door behind them. Walking into the garden, they planned to use the shortcut past the fountain to the stables to meet Wills, who would put their bags in the coach.

"I smell cigar smoke," Barnaby said as he dropped the bags and pulled Mara behind the bushes. They stayed in place, not moving an inch until the Runners patrolling the grounds strolled by.

"We best hurry. The guards should be back in about fifteen minutes. I almost forgot about them." Barnaby picked up the bags again and rushed to the stables.

Wills leaned against the carriage, waiting for them. "Let me have your bags. I can stow them. Seems many people be on patrol tonight."

"How many have you seen?"

"Two Runners and two of Mr. Graham's men. I heard them say they would meet by the fountain in the center of the garden. You got about ten minutes."

"Thank you, you have been such a great conspirator," Mara said.

"I be a what?"

"A great help to us."

Barnaby reached out and handed the young man an envelope. "We appreciate your assistance."

Mara and Barnaby ran back the way they came and were back in the kitchen seconds before they heard the Runners moving around the side of the house.

"We timed our walk in the dark to perfection." Barnaby grinned.

"I know nothing about timely. I do know we were lucky. How about a drink before we turn in?" She reached for his hand. "At this moment, I am too excited and nervous about our plans to sleep."

They walked hand in hand to the library. Mara poured the drinks while Barnaby stirred the fire and added coal.

The next morning found both couples in the library eating breakfast.

"Barnaby and I plan to stay at Woodhaven most of the day. Let us meet here late in the day for tea."

"Mara, that's a wonderful idea. Graham and I have errands to run, so the timing should be just about right. See you both later."

Barnaby and Mara stayed in the library, drinking coffee, chatting, and trying to look normal. Both found it harder and harder to do. About the time they thought they would leave, Graham came back for some papers he needed to give to his solicitor.

Finally, Mara suggested they go for a walk in the garden. She said she could not eat or drink anything else, or they would just have to stop every few miles to use the necessary. When it seemed Maggie and Graham had actually left, the lads strolled in.

They came by for some biscuits. After all, it was a baking day for Mrs. Millbe, and she would have packets of sweets ready for them. She always did.

Barnaby sent Hirsch for the carriage. When it pulled up at the front door, two KM6 men arrived at the same time to discuss a new government situation with Barnaby.

Before they left the house, Mara left a note on the ornate table in the foyer addressed to Maggie and Graham explaining their plans. They knew the couple would not be home until tea time, later in the afternoon. Barnaby and Mara were finally on their way to get their hired vehicle. The special license she received two days ago was tucked safely in Mara's carry bag.

Chapter Twenty-Three

Eel made sure Mr. Barnaby and Miss Mara didn't see the boys following them. They stayed far enough back to remain out of sight.

"I know them be up to something. I recognize the look. What did Miss Mara say the other day? Her said she could tell we was up to no good cause of the looks on our faces." Eel grinned as the trio followed the couple.

Due to the traffic, the Woodhaven carriage moved slowly, making it easy for the boys to trail behind them. Eel noticed a man on horseback who appeared to be following the coach. The rider stopped when Wills drove up to the carriage rental stable.

When the man dismounted from his horse, all three of the lads recognized him. Eel poked Jimmy in the ribs, and Jimmy poked Jeb.

"He be the attacker who tried to shoot Miss Mara." Eel pulled Jimmy and Jeb to the side of the nearest building. "We have to watch and see what happens."

Barnaby and Wills removed the bags and put them in a small travel carriage. The young store clerk helped Mara into the coach and stood waiting for Barnaby, who lingered, talking to the owner.

The attacker stood in the doorway of the building across the street and did not move until the rental vehicle pulled into traffic. Wills strolled back to the

Woodhaven carriage where the three lads ran up to him.

"We seen the man who tried to harm Mara in front of her shop. He followed them on a horse."

"You be sure?"

"Yes. You must warn Mr. Barnaby and Miss Mara," Eel said.

"I can. I know they be stopping for their midday meal at a place called the Plum Thicket on the London Road."

Wills hopped on his perch, gathering the reins in his hand.

"We be going to get Mr. Graham. He can meet you," Eel shouted, dashing down the street with his mates right behind him.

The three lads ran back to the Woodhaven Estate. The boys pounded on the massive front door. They all shouted for Hirsch. Jimmy rushed to the garden to see if perhaps he was outside going to the stables. Finally, Eel heard him coming down the stairs talking to Ivy, the maid.

"Hirsch, we must find Mr. Graham and Miss Maggie." Eel jumped in front of the butler. "The man who tried to harm Miss Mara at Creations is following her and Mr. Barnaby."

"What are you talking about? They are—" The lads all started talking at once. Hirsch shouted, "Stop. One of you speak first."

Eel quickly explained what they knew. "Wills said he be going to help Mr. Barnaby and Miss Mara when he catches up to them. Mr. Graham needs to get to the Plum Thicket on the London Road as quick as he can."

Eel and his mates ran to find Maggie. They hurried to her house first. Hirsch agreed to locate Mr. Graham.

Maggie and the lads were the first to arrive back at Woodhaven. She paced the floor in the library. Eel went to the front door. He saw Graham and Hirsch jump down from a market wagon. He beamed from ear to ear when he read whose name was neatly printed on the envelope.

"Miss Maggie, I found this here on the table near the door. It be addressed to you and Mr. Graham."

Hirsch and Graham walked into the room.

"This better be good. I left an important meeting," Graham announced.

Eel wet his lips. "We followed Mr. Barnaby and Miss Mara when them left the house. I knew they be up to something 'cause the way they be acting."

"Eel, get to the point." Graham walked over and took Maggie's hand in his.

"Wills took them to the carriage builder on Bridger Street where them rent coaches."

"They put traveling bags in the back of one of them fancy new carriages. I seen them do it," Jimmy said. "So we run to tell you…sir."

****

Graham took the note from Maggie. He tore open the envelope, read the message, and then handed it back to Maggie.

She read the message not once, but twice.

Dear Maggie and Graham,

Barnaby and I are going to get married. We obtained a special license and plan to go to the next town and find a vicar.

By the time you read this, the deed will be done. We intend to return in a fortnight.

Mara and Barnaby

She leaned against the wall for support as her mind was reeling.

"Maggie, have someone go to the cottage by the pond. Hopefully, some of our men might still be there. Have them follow me."

Graham ran to the stables. He pulled a groomsman off a horse that had just been saddled. "Sorry. It is an emergency."

"He's not been ridden for a bit so he might give you a little trouble," the groom said, picking himself up off the ground and dusting off his trousers.

Graham had not gone two feet before the horse started his dance. First he went right, then left, and then jumped in the air, landing on all four hoofs. Graham hung on tight with his legs. The sudden jarring did not unseat him. Graham frequently enjoyed playing with a horse when he started out on a ride. Today, he did not have time to appreciate the horse's antics. After gathering a tight grip on the reins. He gave the animal a hard jab with his boot heels. The horse settled down and broke into a canter. Graham had just reached the outskirts of the city when he heard horses approach him from behind. He pulled out his pistol in case they were men working with Mara's mysterious man.

Chapter Twenty-Four

Mara and Barnaby enjoyed a pleasant trip. They were pleased with themselves. They had driven out of London without any problems. The new carriage proved to be an innovative design. The carriage springs allowed the passengers to sit up higher, which offered a smoother ride. The leather interior seats were bigger and had more padding, which provided more comfort as well. The side windows were more secure and kept out a great deal of road dust. They were at the Plum Thicket Station before they knew it.

The air smelled fresh and clean compared to London, and there was no yellow haze from burning coal. Barnaby preferred the country to the city any day of the week.

When the stable boy got a hold of the lead horse's bridle, the driver quickly climbed down from his perch. He moved to the carriage door, opened it, and offered his arm to Mara.

"I hope your ride was comfortable as promised. This is the most up-to-date, modern design. It is the best we have ever made."

"Delightful," Mara said.

Barnaby handed the driver some coins when he exited the coach. "Get yourself a meal. We plan to leave in about an hour. We shall come out to the carriage when we are ready to depart."

"I shall be waiting, sir." The man bowed his head and moved over to talk to the stable hand.

As Barnaby opened the door into the bar, they heard a horse and rider come into the yard. The smell of cooked meat and fresh bread caught their attention when they walked into the common room. They ordered the full midday meal consisting of lamb stew, fresh-baked bread, and fruit pie. It proved to be delicious. They ate in silence. As they were finishing, the Woodhaven coach driver came through the back door.

He took one step into the building. He tried to attract their attention by waving his arms. Finally, he took a small pebble he had picked up in his shoe and threw it at Barnaby's back. He watched it sail between the couple. With a splash, it landed in Mara's cup of tea.

They both jumped up from their chairs. Wills moved into the room. The young man hurried to the table. He squatted down in the hopes no one could see him and explained why he had followed them.

Barnaby stopped the barmaid when she came to offer them a fresh drink.

"Miss, is there a private room we might use for a few minutes?"

"For a price, I can find you almost anything you desire." She leaned toward Barnaby and winked.

Mara touched the barmaid's arm. She shook her head and handed her some coins. The woman motioned for them to follow her. They all moved into the back room. She opened a door into a small storage room.

"This is very private. No one should bother you." She held up the money. "This gives you a few minutes of private time." She handed them a small lantern and closed the door.

"The coach be on the back road near to the delivery door at the back," Wills said, rubbing his eyes. "The rider did not see me. I stayed clear of the front of the pub, I did. The rider be standing to one side, watching the front door."

"I do not think the man plans to come into the building. If he does, I have a pistol with me. Mara has one too. Do you have a weapon?"

"I got me knife." Wills frowned. "However, I be an expert with it. Oh, I almost forgot. Eel and his mates went to find Mr. Graham to come and help."

"Let us get you something to eat. We can wait for a time for Graham or leave in the Woodhaven carriage and go back to London. I…"

Mara's shoulders slumped when she realized all her planning was going wrong. She sighed.

Mara and Barnaby walked out of the storage room into the bar and then back to the common room. All the rooms were empty. Wills joined them a few minutes later. The barmaid delivered the young man's meal. He had eaten one forkful of meat pie when Graham and his men entered through the back door.

"About time." Barnaby wiped his hand across his face. "You see anyone out there?"

"One man standing by a carriage, which I assume is your driver. Another man standing by a horse."

"Anyone got a plan?" Barnaby asked.

"I got one," Wills said, just before he took another bite of his meal.

"We are waiting to hear it. The man is not going to wait forever." Graham began to pace.

Wills said in a rush, "Miss Mara and I be about the same height. What if I dress up in her clothes? From a distance, he might not notice. Mr. Barnaby can help me into the coach. We then drive away and you three men follow and put an end to this." He emptied his glass of cider.

Mara motioned the barmaid over. "I have £50 I will give you if you let me use a room upstairs."

"What you people be up to?"

"Come with me. I can see you have a need to know what is going on. Am I right?"

The barmaid nodded her head and then smiled.

Mara and the barmaid went into the storage room, and she explained the dilemma they were facing.

"Rebecca, the barmaid, has agreed to take my place," Mara said. "Doesn't think the young lad would ever fool anyone. He can stay with me."

The women went upstairs and changed clothes. Mara fixed Rebecca's hair. From a distance, everyone agreed they looked alike. Graham and his men slipped out the back door. Barnaby and Rebecca walked across the room. The mystery man had started to enter the building, but when he saw them walking toward him, he backed out and let them pass. He then turned and followed them.

Barnaby and Rebecca were halfway to the rented carriage when the mystery man called out, "I will not be denied, nor do I plan to share any part of my inheritance. My family paid with their lives to possess the mistress's necklace. My great-great-grandmother should have received it from the French King. The old fool died. She was banished from the court. It belongs to my family."

Graham and the men walked out from the side of the building.

"You are under arrest for the attempted murder of Miss Mara Highbridge," Graham shouted "Put down your pistol."

"Never. I shall perish first." He straightened out his right arm to take aim.

Mara and Wills left the pub by the back door. They both crept around the building, looking for a good vantage point from which to watch the action. Mara was first to notice a second man pointing a pistol in the direction of Barnaby and the barmaid. She poked Wills in the shoulder with her elbow. The young man threw his knife just as Mara fired her weapon. The knife plunged into the man's heart, and the bullet hit him in the chest. He crumpled to the ground.

A volley of shots rang out fired by Graham and his men. The man who had followed Barnaby and Mara fell backward and did not move.

"Where did the second man come from?" Mara looked around to make sure there were no others.

Wills pointed to a horse tied to a tree behind the pub. They found no identification on the man. His saddlebags were empty. No one recognized him. At this point, he became another mystery. Neither Barnaby or Graham liked the unknown. Maybe someone in London could identify him.

The men wrapped up both bodies in old sails and placed them in the luggage compartment in the back of the Woodhaven carriage. Wills would drive them back to London and deposit them at the undertaker. Graham took the men's horses to London. He had a plan that would involve the lads.

Rebecca refused to take any money for her part in the deception. "I knew I would be safe. It were a lark. I enjoyed every minute. It be something to tell my children if I ever have any."

"I have a connection to one of the best dress shops in all of London. I will see you receive a new wardrobe for helping us this day."

"Thank you." Rebecca beamed.

While Barnaby and Graham were discussing the events, Rebecca took Mara into the pub and made her a cup of tea. Plum Thicket was devoid of any customers, so the women began to chat.

"I were wondering why you and your man be here. We don't get many couples stopping. This been a place for folks who ain't always honest."

"Barnaby and I are many things. Honesty is the most important part of our lives. We are eloping today. We stopped here for a mid-day meal and became involved in much more than we planned."

"We got a nice church here. The vicar, he be trustworthy and kind. I could be having you meet with him."

"Sounds like a good idea. I do have one question for you."

"Be happy to help."

"Barnaby and I are looking to buy a farm to raise food for a home we have in London for people who have nowhere to live. We also have a school for people of all ages to learn to read and write. We are planning to train people in farming so they can make a living anywhere they wish to go. Do you know of any places for sale hereabouts? This would be an ideal location, being so close to London for transportation and the like."

"Let me find my Da, and he might be able to help you. I may even know the perfect place."

"My name is Mara. Could you first talk to the vicar? Then you can bring your father to discuss the farm that might be for sale."

"Yes, Miss Mara. I be doing just that."

"I shall stay right here and enjoy my tea."

Mara was never one to pass up an opportunity, or at least find out about one. This thinking had brought her some wonderful opportunities, starting with Creations.

Rebecca ran from the table. Before Wills, Graham, and his men left, Mara requested Graham convert some of the diamonds into cash so they could purchase a farm if they found one to their liking while they were on their travels.

"Not to worry. I shall see you have the funds for anything you require. A courier should arrive within three days with all the information you need."

After everyone left, Barnaby joined her. She told him about her conversation with Rebecca.

Barnaby and Mara were married later in the day at a small church in the center of town. Rebecca made them a wedding feast at the Plum Thicket. Afterward, the newlyweds were taken on a tour of a farm. The location proved to be perfect. It would keep transportation costs down, and they could easily continue to run their other businesses in London.

The house and outbuildings were not in the best of shape, but they were fixable, and what was not could be torn down and replaced.

They made an offer, and since the previous owners

had left and never paid Plum Thicket for the farm, Rebecca's father sold it to them at a reduced price. They stayed for three nights at the Plum Thicket and were just getting ready to leave when a messenger arrived with a large envelope. Inside, Mara found money, a letter from the bank authorizing their ability to procure anything Mr. and Mrs. Roget desired, and congratulations from Maggie and Graham.

Mara hired Rebecca to watch over the property and find a few men who would be interested in honest work. Within a month or sooner, Barnaby and Mara would be back to start the cleaning up of their first farming endeavor.

After leaving, they proceeded to the next town. Their hired driver provided some maps. At night they lay in bed and planned where they wanted to tour next. In no time, they discovered there wasn't any form of transportation to get them safely from place to place. The carriage did well in town, but the roads, once leaving the towns, were nonexistent. They were simply tracks in the dirt and were so rutted that if you tried to travel after it rained, you got stuck more often than not.

The newlyweds planned to see Oxford, Bath, and Stonehenge. However, that was not going to be possible. So, they reluctantly gave up their idea of a country tour. In a few years, rail travel would be faster and easier for seeing the historical sites in England.

One night after making love and lying in each other's arms, they decided to tour neighboring farms in the hopes of discovering how to grow successful crops. After traveling to a village or town, Barnaby and Mara stayed in a local pub or rented a room from a homeowner. People were so intrigued by their plans, they made them feel at home. Some even offered to help when the time came to begin farming their land.

Time went by faster than they could have imagined, and they were headed back to London before they knew it. They both hoped nothing would damper their plans. Only time would tell.

Chapter Twenty-Five

Mara felt like a mother hen when it came to the farm. Everyone came to her with questions and guidance, including Barnaby. She really didn't mind as this was a new adventure and one she was proud of. The newlyweds stopped on their way back to Woodhaven to look over the farm and figure out what work would be required to make it habitable. They named it Rogue's Place. Everything was in worse shape than they remembered. But it was all fixable. It would require a tremendous amount of work to make it profitable. This had been the reason for the price being way below market value.

First, the house had to be cleaned and repaired. The previous owners, they discovered, were thieves and had been blockade runners during the Napoleonic Wars. In fact, Barnaby was sure one of the men might have given Graham the drawing of the necklace.

They stayed at the Plum Thicket for a few days. Rebecca introduced them to the workers she had found. Barnaby and Mara interviewed them and made it crystal clear Rogue's Place was to be an honest and respectable farm. A few of the men left, but most seemed happy to have a decent place to work. Barnaby gave them duties to perform until he came back in a week or two. All the workers reported to Rebecca, and of course, a few more left because they were not going to work for a woman.

Graham and Maggie stayed at Woodhaven while Barnaby and Mara were on their wedding trip. Susan managed Creations, and in truth, it didn't seem anyone really missed them. Mara was not sure if she should be pleased or unhappy. In reality, she was glad to be back in London where there was much for the couple to do.

Within a week, Barnaby and Graham were back with the lads and a few other men from Home Sweet Home. They pitched a couple of tents and went to work. The boys brought the two horses Graham had given them. Mara and Maggie followed a week later.

Mara helped the lads purchase an old cart which they repaired and started a hauling business using their newly painted vehicle. She wasn't surprised Eel was in charge. He informed her he would be negotiating their hauling contracts. All profits would be split evenly with his mates. The lads did work for the Plum Thicket and others in the immediate area. Mara made sure Barnaby and Graham promised to teach them the fine art of business. All were eager to learn. The lads still had not given a name to their enterprise but promised Mara they would when they thought of a good one.

Mara and Maggie had never worked so hard in their lives. Their bodies were more tired than they could ever remember being. Their hands were red from cleaning every corner in the old farmhouse. At least it now was habitable. They no longer had to stay in the tents. Both of them had to admit they were enjoying themselves. They hired a cook and two housemaids. In the next week, they planned to go back to London to gather up some furniture. The women had lists upon lists of items to purchase.

The house had just been painted. The entire place

looked once again like a farm. Happy voices came from the porch. Mara stood on a corner of it, just enjoying the scenic view of the land, which at this time wasn't much beyond weeds and more weeds. Still, it belonged to her and Barnaby and in time would be a real farm. Actually, one of many was her hope. Out of the corner of her eye, she noticed a man who appeared to be hiding behind a bush.

She was watching so intently she was surprised when Barnaby touched her shoulder. "I came to get you to look at the shelves in the kitchen. What are you looking at?"

"Someone is hiding in the bush by the fence. Odd, don't you think?"

"No, because I think I might know who he is."

They quietly and carefully made their way toward the man who suddenly stood next to Graham. They got close enough to overhear their conversation.

"About time you showed up, Otus." Graham shook his head. "I thought I saw you earlier in the day. Noticed you on the road, then a few minutes later you were gone. Where have you been? People are looking for you. I guess I should say hunting you. No one in the area offered any information regarding your whereabouts to the authorities. But I figured you would be back, sooner or later."

The man just shrugged. "Not sure why I came back. My hidey-holes in France and England have become less and less available to me. Most of my partners have been killed, arrested, transported, or hanged. I need to leave England and Europe. There is no longer a safe place to hide. My days as a French blockade runner are over, at least in England."

"You know Peter is dead. Died from some disease."

"Yes, someone mentioned it to me. What do you know about the necklace? I need funds to go to the Colonies."

"I cannot help with the necklace. But I can, for old times' sake, give you funds to start a new life."

"Why? You owe me nothing, Graham."

"He may not, but we do."

Both men spun around to see Mara and Barnaby move in their direction.

"I know who and what you are. Because of you, I met a man I wished had been my father. His only fault was he loved my mother, trusted her, and she betrayed him. Barnaby and I can stake you enough money to leave England and start a new life. However, know if you come back, I promise to see you hanged for all your crimes."

"I will take your offer. I lived my life the way I wanted and ain't going to apologize for anything I ever did. You cannot possibly know who I am."

"Oh, I do know who you are because Peter left a journal. It told us his story, yours, and that of the woman who gave me life."

"He would not have done so. He was my faithful servant and friend."

"Otus, you can believe what you like. I have been waiting for your arrival because evil always returns to create havoc." Mara handed a package to Barnaby. "In this packet, there is enough money for you to start a new life. Barnaby and Graham will escort you to a ship in London. Once you board the ship and it sails, the money is yours. Refuse to leave, and you forfeit our gift. Do not make the mistake of returning to England, because you will have a date with the hangman if you do."

Mara stood and watched the three men march to the barn, gather their horses, and leave.

Maggie hurried to Mara. "What are Graham and Barnaby doing with Otus? I know him. He is evil to the core."

"I know what he is. Otus Anders, according to Peter's diary, is my real father. And I see no reason not to believe Peter. He loved my mother and me. He wrote about the three of them in great detail. How they betrayed him, time and time again. I was always the daughter of his heart, and he protected me with his life. He was the reason I reached the duchess when I was only hours old. Reading his diary broke my heart. How I wish I could have made his passing more comfortable, or at least got to say a final goodbye."

"Our men are escorting Otus to a ship so he can leave England forever. Good riddance to bad rubbish!"

"Mara, do you think he will ever come back?"

"If he is fool enough to return, he will be given a choice to face the hangman or me. Believe me, the hangman would be his best option."

Author's Note

The story of "The Affair of the Diamond Necklace" is a true story. As in all fiction, I added people and circumstances to fit Mara's story. There are many variations of this story. Here are some of the facts I uncovered. Enjoy!

In 1772, Louis XV of France commissioned a diamond necklace for Madame du Barry, his mistress. The gift at the time was estimated to cost 1,600,000 livres (approximately $14 million in 2015 USD). The Parisian jewelers took several years and a lot of money to gather a perfect set of diamonds and sapphires. In the meantime, Louis XV died of smallpox, and du Barry was banished from the court by his grandson and successor.

Enter a confidence trickster, Jeanne de Valois Saint-Remy, also known as Jeanne de la Motte. She became the mistress of a Cardinal de Rohan, bishop of Strasbourg. A forger, Retaux de Villette, wrote letters to the Bishop claiming they were from the queen whose signature he forged. He was caught because he signed the letters Marie Antoinette de France. Royalty at that time did not use surnames. It is believed Jeanne's husband secretly took the necklace to London, where it was broken up to sell the large individual diamonds separately.

The cardinal and two others were tried on May 31, 1786, and all the charges resulted in their acquittal. Jeanne, the cardinal's mistress, was condemned to be whipped, branded with a V (for *voleuse*, thief) on each shoulder and sentenced to life imprisonment in the prostitutes' prison at Salpêtrière.

In June the following year, Jeanne escaped from prison disguised as a boy. Her husband was tried in absentia and condemned to be a galley slave. The man who forged the letters was banished.

Most of the men involved in one way or another never received much punishment for any of the crimes they committed in this affair. Only the woman was convicted.

I used the necklace in my story because I love historical facts and enjoy reading about them. Neither the necklace nor any of its parts have ever been found. This timeworn mystery, yet to be solved, is still called "The Affair of the Diamond Necklace."

A replica of the necklace is on display at the Chateau de Breteuil, France, and a picture is on their website.

I hope you enjoyed Mara's story. You can contact me at P.O. Box 8752, Pratt KS 67124. I look forward to hearing from you.

Happy reading!

A word about the author...

Z is married, has two grown children, and three grandsons. She enjoys photography and lives in rural Kansas.

Thank you for purchasing *Mara's Legacy*. I look forward to hearing from you. My web address is:

www.zminor.com

my email address is:

zminor@zminor.com

or you can write to me at:

P.O. Box 8752, Pratt, Kansas 67124.